TOUGH HOMBRE

Brand located the two Han men. They were on foot, leading their horse as they searched the shrubbery. They were both armed, moving quietly as they advanced. They both snapped around when Brand stepped into the open, his revolver already moving to his first target. He shot the taller of the pair first, putting a single bullet through his head. The Chinese had time for a shocked grunt before he hit the ground. His partner was slightly more agile and as Brand shifted his aim, this one threw himself flat. The revolver in his hand made a flat sound, powder-smoke lashing from the muzzle. The bullet cleaved empty air. Brand had changed position the moment he had fired his first shot. As the hammer fell on the Chinese shooter's gun Brand was already crouching, his own weapon lining up. He fired twice, placing the .44 slugs into the Chinese as the man started to rise. The heavy impact kicked the Chinese over and he died staring up at the sky.

Brand took time to gather the reins of the horses the Chinese had left some way back. He led them back to where he had left Angel and told her she could come out from cover. There was a long silence before she finally appeared. She stood in front of him, refusing to meet his gaze.

'*Hell of a way to start the day,*' he said...

The Jason Brand Series by Neil Hunter

Gun for Hire
Hard Case
Lobo
High Country Kill
Day of the Gun
Brotherhood of Evil
Legacy of Evil
Devil's Gold

Forthcoming

The Killing Days
Two Guns North

BRAND 8:
DEVIL'S GOLD

Neil Hunter

HUNTER BOOKS
2009

Brand 8: DEVIL'S GOLD
By NEIL HUNTER
First Edition: February 2009
Copyright © 2009 by Mike Linaker

ISBN: 978-0-9561525-0-3

Names, characters and incidents in this book are fictional, and any resemblance to actual events, locales, organizations, or persons living or dead is purely coincidental.
All rights reserved. No part of this book may be reproduced or transmitted in any form or by any means, electronic or mechanical, including photocopying, recording or by any information or storage and retrieval system, without the written permission of the author, except where permitted by law.
This is a HUNTER BOOKS publication
Published by www.lulu.com
Visit the author at www.neilhunterworld.com
Cover image © Dreamstime.com

One

'Your trouble is not being able to relax,' Frank McCord said. He had been watching Brand pace up and down the hotel room for almost ten minutes and his patience had almost run out. 'Remind me sometime to ask Kito to show you his methods for relaxation.'

'The only methods that Oriental son of a bitch knows are designed to cripple and maim,' Brand said.

He was tired of waiting and tired of the place in which he was doing that waiting. The Windsor Hotel had the reputation of being Denver's most prestigious edifice. None of those statistics impressed Brand. The fact that its three hundred rooms boasted gas lighting, and a large percentage of them also had bathrooms, meant less than nothing to him. The hotel was like the city itself. Denver had gone soft, Brand reckoned. He had been in the city long enough to take a look at the ornate gas lamps along its paved streets. He had seen the electric streetcars and the new telephones. None of those inventions eased his feeling of discomfort. Once or twice he had found himself wishing he hadn't returned to Washington with the man McCord sent to find him at Sarita's place. Barely three weeks had passed since Brand's return from the affair of Nante's runaway Apaches. On his return to Washington Brand found himself preparing to leave after a couple of days. Frank McCord had accompanied him on the long train ride to Colorado where they had now been for the last three days.

They were waiting for someone. McCord refused to say who. In fact he had told Brand very little. McCord seemed to have things on his mind and Brand left him to his thoughts.

'Why don't you go for a stroll?' McCord suggested. 'Find yourself a bottle and a woman for a few hours.'

Brand poured himself a fresh cup of coffee. 'What? And miss all the fun going on here?'

'If nothing else your unofficial spell of leave seems to have sharpened your sense of humor.'

Staring at him over the rim of his cup Brand wondered, not for the first time, just how deeply McCord had been involved in the Apache problem with Nante and Benito. Something in McCord's manner hinted that he knew a damn sight more than he was saying. Brand would not have been surprised to learn that McCord had worked the whole deal. The man employed any and all kinds of devious methods to achieve results, and that included working behind the backs of the people who did his dirty work for him.

A sharp rap on the door brought McCord out of his chair. He opened the door to admit a gray suited figure. Brand took a second, and longer look before he realized who he was facing.

'Hello, Jason.'

Brand took the outstretched hand of his old friend Colonel Alex Mundy. He took a critical look at Mundy's outfit and nodded.

'You look better in a suit than I do.'

Mundy smiled. 'Still wearing black, Jason. Maybe I should give you the name of my tailor.'

'Black suits his moods,' McCord said.

They sat down and for a moment there was a strained silence. McCord cleared his throat and Brand glanced at him out the corner of his eye. Maybe now he would get to know what all the secrecy had been about.

'Alex, I think you had better begin,' McCord suggested.

Brand turned his attention to Mundy, aware that this was for his benefit.

'This affair began back in 1864,' Mundy said. 'The Confederacy was hard at work behind the scenes trying to raise money to buy equipment and time. A group of Southern sympathizers in California, mainly mine owners, rallied support and pledged so much of their gold to the Confederacy. Apparently the response they received was overwhelming. By the time they were ready to ship their gold they had close on two-million dollars worth. It was melted into ingots and loaded on a wagon. A group of Confederates, posing as migrants, took the wagon across country. Its destination was Texas. At the coast it would have been put aboard a ship bound for Europe. There the gold would have been used to buy arms and equipment. The Union Army heard about the shipment and sent out patrols across the Southwest to intercept it. One patrol did locate the wagon. According to reports there was a fight and the Confederates died to a man. The reports also stated that the Union patrol was hit later by Apaches. Only three men out of six survived.'

'*The gold?*'

Mundy shrugged. 'Supposedly lost during the fight with the Apaches.'

Shifting his gaze from Mundy to McCord, Brand waited for a continuance. He knew there had to be more. Mundy's story had no conclusion.

'You don't believe the Apache connection?'

McCord shook his head.

'The Army was suspicious at the time but they had nothing solid. And remember there was a war going on. So the matter was left until later. Even after the war there was too much to settle. Nothing was done then.'

'But not forgotten? Even after more than twenty years?'

'The Army never forgets,' Mundy said. 'The three men who supposedly survived the Apache attack had their names kept on file. They didn't know it but a close watch has been kept on their movements. But during the intervening years nothing significant happened. Until recently.'

'Over the last few weeks two of the survivors have died,' McCord went on. 'Both were murdered, and everything points to the third survivor as the killer. We have also discovered that one of the soldiers reported killed by the Apaches was still alive until a week ago. Now he is dead – again murdered.'

'Jason, from what we've been able to put together, it appears the Apache attack was pure fabrication. Three of the Union squad were shot by their own companions and the gold stolen. It was hidden and three survivors came back with their Apache story. Then they were sent back to their units, intending to return at a later date for the gold.'

'So why all the delay?' Brand queried.

'Were still making educated guesses,' McCord said. 'But think about the man left for dead. Shot by his so-called friends and deserted. He must have watched them leave with the wagon and hide the gold. He must have been a bitter man. Wanting revenge. A good way of getting it would have been for him to move the gold to another location. Which only he knew about.'

'So when the others come back looking for the gold it had gone.' Brand glanced at Mundy. 'If this man wanted revenge why didn't he take his story to the Army? A witness could have had those three hung for murder and the gold recovered.'

'Perhaps he decided he'd paid the price and the gold was his. No way we can read what's in a man's mind. Whatever the reason he did not come back. We now know he changed his name and moved to another part of the territory. He even married, though his wife is dead now. But there is a daughter.'

'So we know how it all started. What about the present?'

'This man – McAdam was his name – must have been recognized by one of the original squad. It must have been a shock for them to find there was a witness to what they'd done. It would not have taken them long to put two and two together and connect his being alive to the disappearance of the gold.'

'They go after him and try to get the location of the gold from him. Something goes wrong and McAdam dies.'

McCord nodded. 'One other thing. Only one of the three survivors went after McAdam. Both his partners in crime were recently found dead. And not from natural causes.'

'Sounds a pleasant character.'

Mundy spoke up.

'His name is Harvey Ruger. Forty-two years old. Been on the fringes of the criminal world since he left the Army after the war. He has ideas about moving up the criminal ladder. For a good few years he's been in close touch with organized crime groups. Those based mainly in California. San Francisco and the Barbary Coast. They are beginning to expand and he wants to go with them. Unfortunately Ruger is a gambler. A bad one. He owes a great deal of money. If he could get his hands on that gold shipment he could pay off his debts and buy his way into the criminal fraternity.'

'Has he found it yet?'

Mundy shook his head.

'I don't believe he has. The daughter, Jenny McAdam, vanished right after her father died. Ruger has been spotted in the area. He's probably still looking for her. It could be she knows something about the gold. It could get her killed, too.'

'Any ideas where she might be?'

McCord nodded. 'Perhaps. We have one lead for you. Town of Jubillo, New Mexico. Jenny McAdam has family in the area.'

'Just what are we after here? The gold? Ruger? The girl?'

'All that,' McCord said. 'And more. I have a suspicion that Ruger's plans for the gold involve more than just a few West Coast criminals. I've been in touch with the British. We've exchanged information and it's possible there could be a connection between matters both sides have been investigating. What I want you to do is locate Ruger, and if he finds the gold, see if you can follow it to its destination. Try to curb your natural enthusiasm to shoot everyone until you're able to establish where the gold is going.'

Brand ignored the jibe as he got up.

'And then?'

'Put an end to it,' McCord said. He handed Brand a folder. 'This should give you the information you need.'

'I'll be in touch,' Brand said. He nodded in Mundy's direction and left the room.

McCord poured a couple of shots of whisky, handing one to Mundy.

'You think I'm too hard on him?'

Mundy smiled. 'You know your job. And I think you know Jason.'

'There are times when I'm not so sure. He's a complex character, Alex. I use him the only way I know how. Send him on the kind of assignment that calls for unique talents. Like this one. We have certain facts. A number of leads that need bringing together. Brand will make that happen. He has the knack of making things happen. He creates all kinds of havoc along the way, but he gets results. And we're not in the peace and love business. I don't believe in using a glass hammer to knock in iron nails, Alex. Brand is a hard man. Used to a degree of violence that would turn a lot of men pale. The thing is he can still function, despite the things that have happened to him. He's adapted to a way of life he hates most of the time. The day he turns against it is the day he stops being useful to me. Until then I want him working for me because he's the best I've ever had, but for God's sake, Alex, don't ever let him know I said it.'

Two

Climbing down from the stage Brand felt his boots sink into the soft mud of the street. He waited until the driver passed down his bag, with his rifle strapped to the side then tramped across the street in the direction of the building advertising itself as a hotel. He hunched his shoulders against the cold wind and rain coming down from the clouded New Mexico sky. He was chilled from the long hours he had endured in the creaking coach. Hunger gnawed at his stomach and tiredness stung his eyes. One way and another it was a hell of a way to start an assignment.

He stepped up onto the slippery verandah, kicking sticky mud from his boots. Though it was barely evening lamps were being lit against the premature gloom. Brand went through the door into the hotel lobby. It was warm if nothing else, the heat coming off a glowing stove in one corner. He crossed to stand in front of it, grateful for the comfort it offered. He unbuttoned his shortcoat, stamping his feet on the floor to aid the circulation.

'Hell of a day to be traveling, friend.'

Brand glanced over his shoulder in the direction of the speaker, and saw a woman leaning on the reception desk. She had a half smile on her lips and a bold gleam in her eyes. He made his way over to the desk. The woman handed him a pen and he signed his name in the book. He could feel her eyes still on him.

'Single room?' she asked, making even that sound like a challenge.

Brand nodded.

'I'll let you have number four. It's on the front. Right over mine, as a matter of interest.'

'I'll keep that in mind,' Brand told her.

The woman straightened up. He saw she was tall, around thirty years old and though was not beautiful she possessed a sensual personality that reached out to make itself known. Brand found himself taking note of her physical qualities as she stepped out from behind the desk. The snug gray dress she wore appeared to have been designed to emphasize the full breasts while not detracting from her small waist and curving hips.

'Can I get a meal somewhere?' Brand asked.

She nodded. 'Few doors down there's an eating house. They serve good food. Nothing fancy but plenty of it.'

'Just how I like it.'

She handed him his room key. 'That apply to other things?'

Brand smiled. 'Never know your luck, ma'am.'

'The name's Connie, Mister Brand. Day I let a man call me ma'am I'll know I'm getting old.'

'Mind if I leave my bag down here? If I don't eat first I won't make the stairs.'

Connie nodded and took his bag. She slid it out of sight behind the desk.

'I'll make sure there are clean sheets put out for you,' she said. 'Always make sure my guests are comfortable in bed.'

Connie, Brand said to himself, *I'm damn certain you do*.

He left the hotel and made his way along the street. He found the eating house and went inside. It was small but looked clean and inviting. Brand found he was the only customer. He chose a table by the front window, took off his coat and sat down. A slender, dark eyed girl took his order, bringing him the pot of coffee he had asked for straight away. Brand poured himself a cup. It tasted good. After the food and drink he'd been suffering for the past few days, even the worst coffee in the world would have been gratefully received.

He thought back over the long hours he'd spent traveling from Denver. First by train, then three different stage lines, to this small town in Northwest New Mexico. It was called Jubillo and it sat on a rise above the San Juan River. Nothing special as far as Brand was concerned, except that a few miles beyond town lived the only relatives of the girl known as Jenny McAdam. There was no proof the girl had actually gone to stay with her kin. She was alone, frightened, and she had gone on the run. Despite it being a thin chance Brand had decided it was one worth taking. He had found out from past experience that when people were in trouble and needed somewhere to hide they most often chose familiar ground. There was also the consideration that the man called Ruger might have discovered the girl had family. If Ruger was as smart McCord had implied he wouldn't pass up checking such an obvious refuge himself.

When his meal came Brand ate well. The food was plentiful and better cooked than he had expected. The steak that filled his plate was rich and tender. It was accompanied by boiled potatoes and greens. There were fresh baked biscuits and gravy made with the juice from the meat. A second pot of coffee rounded off the meal. Brand paid his bill and left. He turned up the collar of his coat against the chill. The rain had stopped but the temperature was still down. Brand took a slow walk around town, partly to exercise off the meal, but also to give himself a chance to look the town over. There was not a great deal to see. Jubillo looked like it existed to service the passengers from the various stage lines that crisscrossed the territory. When he spotted a saloon he decided to take a drink. That was secondary to the main reason for going in. Saloons served as clearing houses for a great deal of information.

Brand pushed open the door and stepped inside. The smell of liquor and tobacco smoke wafted through the motionless air as he closed the door behind him. He crossed to the bar, ignoring the curious stares. He had already made a mental note of the occupants. Eight of them – including the red faced individual behind the counter.

'Beer,' Brand said. He dropped some coins on the sticky counter. He had seen better places.

'Passin' through?' the bartender asked. He slopped Brand's glass of beer in front of him.

'Looking for someone.'

The bartender almost twitched with interest. He leaned closer, his eagerness to please causing sweat to pop out across his face. 'Maybe I can help.'

Brand lifted his beer and took a swallow. 'Could be. I'm not expecting to get my answers for nothing.'

The bartender almost fell off the edge of the counter. He scrubbed a wrinkled hand across his nose. 'I'm listening.'

'Could be a couple of people I'm interested in. Man called Ruger. Should be in his early forties. Other's a girl. She'd be on her own. Around eighteen. Likely be on the nervous side. Name of Jenny McAdam.'

The bartender thought for a moment. 'Can't help you with the man. But I might know the girl...'

'Wally don't know a damn thing, mister, so I were you I'd not ask him any more questions.'

Brand eased around to stare at the speaker. He saw a tall, broad-bodied man. A strong, hostile face. There were two others behind him.

'Back off, fellers, no need to crowd me. Plenty of room along the bar.'

'Could be you ought to finish that drink and come outside.'

'I'm going to finish the beer,' Brand said. 'Not so sure I'm interested in going outside with you. I generally leave when I'm ready.'

The hostile face darkened with anger. 'Mister, you leave when I say so. And I say now.'

Brand saw the fist coming and made to duck away from it. The edge of the bar stopped him. The fist missed his jaw. The follow-up blow clouted him alongside his head. The punch pushed Brand along the edge of the counter, his arm catching his glass of beer and knocking it to the floor. The sound of breaking glass reached Brand through a hiss of noise as he shook his head. The blow had stunned him for a few seconds. It was long enough for clawing hands to grab at his clothing and haul him away from the bar. Hard fists slammed into his body, their effect lessened by the thick coat he was wearing. Brand knew that eventually his body would lose its capacity for punishment. Before that happened he needed to gain some advantage for himself. He didn't understand the reason behind the unprovoked attack and at this moment he didn't care. That could come later. He concentrated on the now and hit back. Planting both feet hard against the floor Brand thrust forward, driving his shoulder against the closest body. Proof of his contact came when a man grunted in pain. Brand kept pushing, feeling the man give way. He saw an angry face rising in front of him and he slammed his fist into it. Blood spurted from split lips. The man shook his head, spraying more blood. This time Brand punched him low in the stomach. Hard. The man yelped and sagged to his knees and Brand smashed a hard boot heel across the side of his upturned face. As the man rolled aside Brand felt powerful arms wrap themselves around his body. He twisted violently but the arms maintained their hold. The third man appeared in front of Brand his face twisted with anger as he smashed a hard knuckled fist across Brand's jaw. The blow landed with a solid impact. Brand's head seemed to explode with pain. It felt as if the side of his face had been ripped off. For a few seconds he blacked out and when he could see again the same fist was raised before his eyes. He drove his heels into the floor and kicked back. Heard the man behind him grunt with the effort as he tried to keep Brand imprisoned in his arms. Then the man's back was slammed up against the edge of the bar. Ribs cracked and pain edged the man's exclamation. His grip slackened and Brand yanked himself free. He stepped forward to meet the forward rush of the man in front of him, brushing aside the fist swinging at his head and drove in swift punches of his own, putting every ounce of his anger in the crunching blows that knocked the other man back. Helpless under the onslaught the man pawed the air as he tried to defend himself. Brand overcame the resistance and kept up his attack until the man stumbled and fell to the saloon floor, gasping and spitting blood.

Brand opened his coat and pulled out his Colt. He stepped away from the bar until he was able to cover all three of the bloody figures. He heeled a chair close and sat down, watching them. His face and body throbbed with pain and he spat blood from his aching mouth. He caught the attention of the bartender.

'Hey, Wally, whisky. Make it a large one.'

The bartender nodded. He poured the drink and brought it over. Brand took it in his left hand, noticing that his knuckles were already starting to swell. He downed the whisky.

'You know these boys?' he asked the bartender.

Wally nodded. 'The McAdams.'

'Jesus,' Brand muttered.

He had come all the way from Denver to find these people and had ended up brawling with them. Not that they had given him much choice in the matter. He wondered sourly why it was nothing ever ran smoothly in his life. No matter how a man wished things to happen there was always something liable to cause upset.

He glanced up to see the one who had first spoken to him standing a few feet away. The man's face still held a sullen expression but it was also bruised and bloody now. It gave Brand a small degree of satisfaction.

'Ease off there, mister,' Brand warned. 'No damn call for us to fight. Believe it or not I'm here to help you.'

The man wiped blood from his mouth. 'You was askin' about Jenny,' he said. 'We've had enough trouble without you bastards chasin' that girl all over creation. Hell, man, she needs to be left alone.'

'There've been others?' Brand was suddenly very interested. 'How many?'

'Only two of 'em...hell, I ain't wastin' my time tellin' you all I know,'

'Be a deal less painful than the way we've been talking up to now.'

'Look, mister, who the hell are you? And what is this all about?'

Three

'After what happened to Jenny's old man, and with her running scared, we got past askin' too many questions,' Tom McAdam said slowly, favoring the swollen lip Brand had given him.

'Hell, Tom, how do we know this sonofabitch is who he says he is?'

Brand glanced across the table at the speaker. Ned McAdam was young and full of youthful belligerence. He made no attempt to conceal his suspicions about Brand.

'I don't give a damn if you believe me or not,' Brand said. 'I've told you why I'm here. My business is with Jenny McAdam. To help her. Don't stand in my way, boy, or I'll finish what you started tonight.'

'Ned, back off.' This time there was a hard edge to Tom McAdam's words. He looked beyond Ned's angry face to where the third McAdam brother leaned against the bar nursing a beer. 'Just go see if Ed is all right.'

Ned leaned forward, his face darkening. He threw a murderous glance in Brand's direction, eyes challenging, but when he received no response he thrust to his feet and went across to the bar.

'He figures he's tough,' Tom McAdam said, almost apologetic.

'He'll learn,' Brand replied. 'One way or the other.'

'I wish *I* could learn what this all about,' McAdam snapped. 'Hell, man, surely you can tell me?'

'The less people who know the better,' Brand said. He had no intention of revealing his assignment to McAdam. There was no need. Once he had an answer to his questions he would be finished with Tom McAdam and his brothers. 'Where is she?'

McAdam stared at the tabletop. He fiddled with his whisky glass. Finally he looked up, fixing his stare on Brand's face.

'About a day's ride south of here there's a line of hills. At one end is a high peak. Has a bald crest. Halfway up the west slope is a canyon that runs into the center of the peak. There's a cabin an' all. Jenny's hiding there.'

Brand drained his glass. 'Thanks for that,' he said. 'We could have done this without the bruises.'

Tom McAdam raised his glass. 'What the hell.'

Stepping outside Brand sucked in cool, fresh air. He winced as pain flared over his ribs. He was going to be stiff come morning. He crossed over to the hotel.

In the morning he would have to rent a horse and go look for Jenny McAdam. The prospect did little to cheer him up. New Mexico was big country, and even though he had been born in the territory, covering much of it over the years, he was aware he could very easily find himself in difficulty. But that was tomorrow and it could wait. All he needed right now was his room and his bed.

He had almost forgotten about the woman called Connie. But she hadn't forgotten him. He was halfway up the stairs when he became aware of being watched. She was waiting for him at the top, leaning against the wall. The gray dress had been exchanged for a thin, clinging robe.

'Heard you got yourself into a little trouble.'

Brand couldn't help smiling. 'News travels fast around here.'

'Small town.'

'Life is just one round of fun and games.'

Connie smiled. 'I heard that too. You got any damage that needs tending. Aches and pains?'

She followed him to his door, waiting while he unlocked it, then followed him inside. Brand closed the door. He peeled off his coat, biting back against the sore ribs.

'Just what went on over to the saloon?' Connie asked. 'Way I heard it you and the McAdam boys had a real set to.'

Brand took off his shirt and examined himself in the mirror over the wash stand.

'Just a misunderstanding,' he said.

Connie laughed. 'You often have that kind of misunderstanding?' she asked.

'From time to time.'

She stared at him, not failing to notice the scars laced across his hard torso. 'Once in a while?' she repeated softly. When Brand turned towards her she asked, 'Hey, you want to see *my* scars?'

'This all part of room service? Or have I won a local raffle?'

Connie shook her head. 'No. I learned a long time ago that life's too damn short to waste. And if I take a liking to someone I can't see the sense in passing up the opportunity for a little break in the routine. You'd be surprised how lonely it gets in a place like this.'

'You? Lonely? Can't believe that.'

'My problem is I'm choosy.'

Brand went to her, his resolved weakening before her blatant invitation. Before he reached her Connie let the robe slip to the floor and he caught a glimpse of her full-breasted nakedness before she pushed against him, pressing her soft lips against his.

What followed was still hazy in Brand's mind when he opened his eyes the next morning. The curtains had been opened and brilliant sunlight streamed into the room. He sat up slowly. His head ached dully and the pain over his ribs was still there. He staggered from the bed to the wash stand. Poured water into the basin and soaked his face and head until the nagging ache subsided. Then he had an all-over wash, dried himself and got dressed. The dark suit was packed away and he dressed in faded Levi's and a dark shirt. He pulled on his socks, then stomped his feet into his boots. Sitting on the edge of the bed he checked his revolver and the Henry rifle he had brought with him. He made certain both weapons were fully loaded.

Downstairs he found Connie behind the desk, going through a stack of paperwork. She glanced up as he appeared and handed her his room key.

'You leaving us?'

'I'll be back for my gear,' he said.

'I look forward to that. Anything in particular you found to your liking?'

Brand smiled. 'Room service was of a very high standard.'

'Yes it was. How long you going to be away?'

'I don't know.'

Connie watched him cross the lobby and step outside. He paused for a moment, getting his bearings, and then he was gone. She stared at the empty doorway for a long time. *Wasn't that the way it always ended?* Men who came and went, leaving her alone. Except for the memories. She tried to push her thoughts of Brand to the back of her mind, concentrating on the paperwork. The problem was forgetting didn't come easily when it came to someone like Brand. Surprisingly she found herself blushing at her recall of what had happened the previous night, and she finally admitted that the memory of that was something she did not want to lose too quickly.

After a good breakfast Brand sought out the livery stable. It was at the far end of town, a two story wooden building fronted by high double doors. The owner was a squat, broad Dutchman who looked slow on his first appearance. He turned out to be far from that. He was a canny horse trader. He dickered for every cent involved in the hiring of a good horse and saddle. Even so Brand came away knowing he had made a good deal. He rode his newly acquired animal up the street to a general goods store where he stocked up on food and cooking utensils.

Leaving town Brand cut off south and gave his frisky horse its head for a time, letting it blow off steam. The air was fresh after the previous day's rain and the heat was back.

He had a good ride ahead of him and he used it to do some thinking. To consider what might be in store for him. Tom McAdam had told him two men had been in Jubillo looking for Jenny. The moment she had found this out the girl had quit the McAdam place for the hideaway in the nearby hills. That had been two days ago. Ample time for the men looking for her to have picked up her trail. For all Brand knew Jenny McAdam might already be in their hands. Or dead. The people involved had already shown what they were capable of. They were the kind who would kill at the slightest provocation. They had no remorse. No consideration for the suffering they caused. They were hard, uncompromising men. The thought of Jenny McAdam in their hands concerned Brand.

He rode all that day and at dusk he was able to see the hills on the horizon. He kept riding until full dark forced him to stop. There was no moon and the few stars offered little in the way of guiding light. Brand made camp in a dry wash, building his fire beneath a rocky overhang. He fried himself a couple of slices of thick bacon and warmed up some of the beans he'd purchased. While he waited for his coffee to brew he pulled on his thick coat as protection against the chill. He ate his solitary meal and drank his coffee. When he had finished he lit a thin cigar and sat with his back to a solid chunk of weathered rock.

It took a while for him to get comfortable. His steady riding had not done a deal to ease the mild discomfort he still felt after the fight with the McAdams. His face was sore too and he allowed he was going to have to go without shaving for a day or so to give it time to heal up.

In the morning he would start looking for tracks. He would soon know if Jenny McAdam had been around here and if she had been followed. Later he checked his horse, unrolled his blanket and settled for the night. Before sleep claimed him he admitted it had been a sight more comfortable sharing his bed with Connie.

He woke early, rolling out of his blanket and clearing his camp site while a fresh pot of coffee brewed. He had his couple of cups, emptied the pot and saddled up. Moving off he scanned the hills he was nearing and studied the ground for tracks. He had been in the saddle for an hour and was just negotiating the foothills when he spotted a rider. Brand pulled his Henry rifle from the saddle-sheath and levered a round into the breech. As he brought his horse around he recognized the rider.

It was Tom McAdam.

'That's a sure way of getting yourself shot at,' Brand snapped, lowering the rifle.

'You picked up any trail?' McAdam asked. He stood in his stirrups, searching the way ahead.

'Nothing yet.'

Brand fished out a fresh cigar and matches. He lit the cigar and studied McAdam. The man was jumpy, obviously concerned over some matter.

'They were at the house again,' McAdam said abruptly.

'When?'

'Yesterday. Still askin' after Jenny. When they realized we weren't hiding her they lit out. Looks like they headed in this direction. I didn't find out until I got back. I left the others back to home and took out after you. Figured this was where you'd be heading.'

'*Damn*,' Brand said. He scanned the slopes that rose in front of him. 'They could be anywhere up there. Could have picked up Jenny's trail by this time.'

McAdam struggled to form his next words.

'I'd like to go along with you, Brand. We give you a hard time yesterday. We were wrong and I figure I owe you. Another gun could come in handy.'

'You know these hills?'

'Damn right I do.'

'You want to be useful get me to that hideaway by the quickest route you know.'

Tom McAdam nodded. He yanked on the reins, turning his horse and set off along the base of the slope. Brand followed as they rode McAdam's unmarked trail for almost a mile. Without warning McAdam started up the slope. Brand realized McAdam hadn't been exaggerating his knowledge of the hills. He seemed to know every rock and clump of brush, every hidden gully and hump. They rode for uppermost of two hours, their horses lathered and winded. And then McAdam drew rein. He hunched round in his saddle as Brand eased alongside. McAdam pulled off his hat and sleeved sweat from his face.

'Jesus, it's hot,' he grumbled.

Brand wasn't about to argue. The open aspect of the hills offered little cover from the hard beat of the sun. He could feel his own shirt clinging damply to his back.

'We stopping for a reason?' he asked McAdam. 'Or is it just to pass the time of day?'

McAdam managed a smile. 'You're a hard son of a bitch, Brand, I'll give you that.' He raised a hand and pointed. 'See there. Where the bald peak starts. At the base is the way up to the canyon.'

Brand followed his direction and picked out the dark split in the hardrock. The entrance to the hideaway. He just hoped they weren't too late.

It took another hour to reach the entrance to the canyon. Close up it turned out to be wider than he had imagined. At the opening Brand reined in, studying the dusty ground.

McAdam swore when he spotted what had caught Brand's attention. Faint tracks in the dust where a single rider had entered the canyon. The hoof prints were a few days old. But now fresher prints, of two horses, could been seen overlaying the first.

'Not been made long,' McAdam said.

'No more than an hour.'

Brand pushed his horse into the canyon. It ran in a straight line for a couple of hundred yards, then curved off to the right, widening as it leveled out again.

'How far does it run?'

'A half mile.'

As they neared the end of the defile it opened out into the large, natural basin where the cabin stood. Brand eased to a stop. He dismounted and tethered his horse. McAdam joined him.

'The cabin's to the left. Just beyond those trees.'

Brand moved through the heavy brush that dotted the area. He made his way through the stand of timber until he was able to see the cabin. There was lean to tacked on one side. An unsaddled horse stood in the shade. Two more horses, both saddled, had been tied to one of the lean to's uprights.

'Damn,' McAdam muttered. 'Those belong to the two been askin' about Jenny.'

'Well it looks like they found her.'

The silence of the canyon was abruptly shattered by a woman's scream. It was a high, agonized sound. The sound of someone in terrible pain.

'*Christ*,' McAdam said. 'Jenny, I'm comin', girl.'

His action took Brand by surprise. He had no chance of stopping McAdam bursting into the open and running towards the cabin.

'Leave her alone, you bastards.'

Brand swore out of pure frustration. *Damn McAdam.* The man was asking for trouble. He was going to get himself...

The sound of the shot drowned out McAdam's yelling. The bullet hit him in the left shoulder and spun him round. For a split second he stared directly at Brand. Then three more shots rang out. The bullets ripped into McAdam, blowing out through his chest in bloody sprays. McAdam plunged face down on the ground.

Brand had seen the dark shape of the shooter at the window of the cabin. Even as McAdam was falling Brand raised his rifle, aimed and fired at the figure behind the muzzle flashes. He saw the shooter jerk away from the window. Breaking cover Brand angled off towards the far end of the cabin, seeking the shelter of the lean to. He almost made it. With only a few yards to go he saw the cabin door swing open. There was a blurred impression of a tall, dark clad figure moving into the open.

'I'll see to him, Ruger,' the man yelled as he moved forward.

Brand took a dive to the ground. He grunted as his ill-timed move shocked the breath from his body when he landed. He kept himself moving, gasping for breath, rolling into the cover of the lean to. Behind him a gun went off and he felt the snap of the bullet tear his shirt. He found himself under the hooves of the horses and struggled to maintain control of his movements. As he dragged himself to a sitting position he saw the legs of the advancing gunman. Brand fired, missing by inches.

The target paused, then darted to one side. The delay allowed Brand to gain his feet. He pushed by the nervous horses and with abrupt suddenness found himself face to face with the man who was trying to kill him.

The man almost succeeded. He was quick to react. The heavy revolver in his hand swung in Brand's direction, exploding with sound. The bullet seared a stinging line across the back of Brand's gun hand. He ignored the pain, concentrating on his own shot, knowing it might be the only one he got. He had already spotted the bloody stain on the man's shoulder. His shot through the cabin window had not been wasted. Touching the trigger Brand felt his rifle lift in recoil. His bullet knocked dust from the other man's dark shirt. He saw the blossom of red appear over the man's heart. The dark clad man stepped back. He paused and then sat down on the ground with an awkward motion. He seemed reluctant to give in but after a few seconds he fell over on his side, his head thumping heavily on the hard ground.

Brand ran for the cabin. He knew there was a second man but his priority was the girl. As he neared the open door he leaned his rifle against the outside wall and eased his Colt from its holster. He could see inside the cabin – and the first thing he saw was the naked figure of a young woman suspended by her wrists from one of the roof beams. Brand got a swift impression of white flesh and a lot of blood. The woman's face was turned in his direction, mouth opening as she began to scream again. Brand picked up a soft sound off to his left. He turned, trying to move away from the source of the sound. He was too slow. Something smashed across his skull. The blow sent him reeling and he slammed against the wall. Sickness welled up inside him and he tried to push himself clear of the wall. His strength had slipped away. Brand stumbled awkwardly, pain blossoming inside his skull. He could feel something wet streaming down the side of his face. Somewhere far off he could still hear the girl screaming. He wished the hell she would stop. A shadow danced in front of his eyes. He tried to focus on it. The shadow sprang into focus and Brand stared into the dark, angry face of a wild man, hair falling across a broad forehead. The features were strong, mouth wide open to show large square teeth in a snarl of rage. Brand had no time to react before he was struck a second blow. It drove down across his skull and Brand was sure it had smashed through the bone. The cabin flared with bright light that quickly faded into darkness. He felt himself falling. He never recalled when he hit the floor because his whole world closed down around him and he knew no more.

Four

Jason Brand's anger was directed more at himself than at anything else. He had allowed himself to be taken like a damn tenderfoot straight off the stage, and that thought hurt a sight more than the crack on his head. He knew he was lucky to be alive. He could have walked straight into a bullet. The fact he was still alive puzzled him. The only explanation he could see was that the surviving killer had panicked, perhaps believing there were others following close on Brand's heels and had simply hit him on his way out. Whatever the reason Brand considered he had got off easy.

It took him some time to recover from the heavy blow. When he had come round enough to be able to move Brand had made his cautious way to the shallow stream that ran close by the cabin, splashing water on his face. The clear water, chillingly cold, had stunned him, drawing a gasp from Brand. Despite that he plunged his head beneath the surface, feeling it sting as it came into contact with the gash in his scalp. When he had pulled his head up he saw the water running red with blood. His head ached wickedly. He ducked under the water again, then sank back, letting the pain subside. He could feel his body trembling and knew he was suffering from mild shock.

He stayed beside the stream for some time, content to rest and let his body recover. He felt detached from reality, not belonging, and it was confusing. He knew it was an after effect of the savage blow. He rested until he felt confident enough to climb to his feet and return to the cabin.

He saw the sprawled bodies of McAdam and the gunman and was reminded of the savagery that shadowed men wherever they went. They had a knack of bringing violence and death to any place they set foot. He was not slow in accepting he was often as guilty of being a perpetrator of that violence himself.

He stood at the cabin door, unable to tear his gaze from the ugly scene confronting him. In life Jenny McAdam had been young and attractive. The ruined thing hanging naked and bloodily mutilated bore little resemblance to its former, living self. Brand had seen his share of ugly things in his lifetime but the sight of Jenny McAdam, strung up like some abandoned carcass, brought a gut-wrenching sickness to him. He was trying, and failing, to understand the motivation behind a mind capable of doing such things to another human.

But you do know, his inner voice told him. It was all for a pile of gold. For a wagonload of cold, lifeless metal.

He went inside, pulling his knife and cut the ropes holding Jenny McAdam's body to the beam. He carried her across to the low bunk that stood against one of the walls and placed her on it, drawing a blanket over her body. The effort left him weak and sweating and he felt himself swaying. He still needed to recover from that blow to his head.

Brand took some firewood and went back outside where he built a small fire. He located a pot and a tin with coffee in it. He filled the pot from the stream and placed it on some rocks he had laid in the fire. He stood watching the fire for a while, aware of something nagging at him. Finally he turned and went to the cabin, closing the door so he didn't have to think about Jenny McAdam lying in there. While the coffee brewed Brand walked over to the man he had shot and searched his clothing. The man's pockets gave him little. A pipe the man had smoked, the stem broken when he had fallen after Brand's killing shot. In the same pocket was a wad of dark tobacco. The wrapper around it was in Spanish. There was some paper money and a few coins. There were no other items of identification.

Brand took his coffee and squatted beside the fire. His next priority was to pick up Harvey Ruger's trail. The way it looked Ruger was on his way to pick up the gold. Brand felt sure of one thing. If Jenny McAdam had known the whereabouts of the hidden cache she would have given it to Ruger. There was no way she would have hung on to the knowledge after what had been done to her. Unfortunately divulging the secret had not saved her life.

Later, when he felt he could travel Brand dragged the bodies into the cover of the lean to and unsaddled and set free the horses. His thoughts dwelt briefly on Tom McAdam. The man had thrown away his life, out of his depth with the situation, responding with his emotions instead of his head. Brand didn't spend too much time thinking about McAdam. He had been a man full grown and capable of making his own choices. He had chosen wrongly this time and had died for that choice.

It took Brand a couple of hours to pick up the faint trail left by the man who had ridden away from the cabin. Ruger, and it seemed likely it was he, was no fool when it came to hiding his tracks. Brand had to cut back and forth, searching and retracing his way when he lost the trail. It didn't help that his head was still hurting, the ache deep and heavy. It ate at his nerves, pushing him to the edge of anger and that only weakened Brand's concentration.

He noticed that the shadows were lengthening. The day was slipping away fast. Too fast. Brand swore forcibly. He was way behind his man and it didn't look as if he was going to find Ruger's trail that easy to cross.

He needed to find the man's tracks. Sooner rather than later. Before Ruger lost *him* completely.

Five

Harvey Ruger tipped the canteen back, feeling the tepid water trickle down his parched throat. A large measure of whisky would have suited him better but he knew he was going to have to be content with the water for now. The whisky would come later. As would a great deal of other good things. He allowed himself a quick smile as he contemplated his bright future. As he lowered the canteen he found himself looking into the bland face of Sung Shan. He felt his stomach tense, a knot of apprehension forming there. Damned of it hadn't happened again. That sensation of unease when he stared into the man's eyes. Ruger did not trust Sung Shan – there was something about the man he found unsettling. Maybe it was that eternal watchfulness. The unconcealed caution in Sung's cold, yellow eyes. Sung Shan was a man who spent his time watching others. Seemingly indifferent to everything around him. Ruger knew better and the knowledge brought him little comfort.

'You are still uneasy because you did not make certain of killing that man,' Shan said. His voice, as ever, was low, yet it still managed to convey menace.

Ruger hooked his canteen from the saddle horn, gathering his reins.

'He might still be dead,' he said. 'I hit that bastard hard.'

'A moment's caution is worth a lifetime of doubt.'

'One thing I don't need is any more of your Oriental wisdom,' Ruger snapped.

'Mister Ruger, you would have done well to heed my advice. If Chu had been with you we would have obtained all the information we required much faster and with less effort.'

Ruger glanced over Shan's shoulder at the huge, powerful man he knew only as Chu. Shan's constant companion. A silent, threatening figure, Chu reminded Ruger of the nightmares he had as a child. The one where he was pursued by a huge, hulking monster, ever silent and ever frightening. It was the only way he could describe Chu. The Chinese, with his massive bulk and squat, bald head, carried a puckered scar that ran down the left side of his face, pulling down the corner of his mouth in a permanent snarl. The drawn lips exposed Chu's yellowed teeth.

'I got what we needed,' Ruger said defensively.

'I hope so, Mister Ruger. A great deal of time and money has already been expended on this venture.

Failure now would only serve to upset and anger Master Han. That in turn would anger me.'

'Now that's what I like about you, Shan. Your undivided loyalty.'

Sung Shan permitted himself a rare smile.

'As long as we all understand each other,' he said. 'Shall we continue? In the hope that your information proves accurate.'

'No worry there,' Ruger said. 'McAdam told his daughter exactly where he had moved the gold to. It was all in her head. Now it's in mine.'

'Let us hope you can remember it all in detail.'

Ruger nodded. 'Shan, I know this territory blindfold, and I know where the gold is now.'

'Well let's get to it,' a voice grumbled, 'cause it ain't that much fun sittin' out in this sun.'

Ruger hunched around in his saddle and scowled at the speaker. He tried to figure out how he had let himself become involved with Marc Remo and his partner, Lex Dwyer. The trouble was he hadn't had much choice in the matter. Remo and Dwyer were little more than second-rate gunmen, pushed into Ruger's deal by his San Francisco contacts. They were the kind who would have been more at home along the Barbary Coast, in the bars and brothels along the waterfront. They didn't like the job they had been given, but like Ruger they had little say in the matter. To make up for it they spent most of their time bitching about anything and everything. Ruger was looking forward to the time he would be able to part company with them.

'Remo, all you have to do is drive the wagon. I give the orders. You ain't paid to think.'

'Hell, I ain't no damn teamster,' Remo grumbled. He snatched at the reins of the team pulling the heavy wagon.

Dwyer, on the box beside him, leaned across and smiled at his partner.

'Remo, that's the first damn thing you said I agree with.'

'What?'

'You are no damn good at drivin' a wagon. I got the bruises on my ass to prove it.'

Ruger yanked his horse around, driving his heels in hard. He pushed the animal up the steep slope, driving out every thought but the single, most vital one.

Damn them all.

He'd show the whole sorry bunch, by leading them straight to the gold, then he could have the laugh on them. He knew they didn't fully trust his judgment. Sung Shan especially. The Chinese, with his soft manner and his barely concealed threats, tolerated Ruger because he had to. Let them all wait until he delivered the gold as promised. They would have to change their opinion of him then. The closer he got, the more excited Ruger became. He was unable to hold back his feelings. After all these years he was finally going to see that gold again. *His gold.* Two million dollars worth. His. After all the whole scheme had been his idea and he had made sure it was carried through to the letter. Then it had almost collapsed because McAdam had not died way back. Now, after all the time that had passed, Ruger would soon be back in control. This time McAdam was really dead, as were all the others, leaving Ruger in full command. Even after Kwo Han took his percentage for setting up the deal and Ruger had paid off his outstanding debts to the San Francisco people, he was still going to be a rich man. And richer still after he invested his portion in Kwo Han's business venture.

Reaching the top of the slope Ruger waited for the rest of the party. As Sung Shan drew his horse alongside Ruger pointed to the jagged rise of rocky hills ahead of them.

'In there,' he said. 'In a couple of hours you'll be loading that gold onto the wagon.'

Sung Shan merely nodded. He glanced at Ruger's sweating face.

'Tell me, Ruger, does the gold really mean so much to you?'

'You'll never know just how much.'

They moved on into the bleached, bare hills. There was no other sound save that of their passing. Pale coils of dust rose into the air as they traveled. The deeper they got into the rocky mass the closer the heat became. The very air formed a muffling blanket that seemed to hang overhead and smother them.

Midday had come and gone when Ruger brought them to the bottom of a deep depression. A high rock wall sloped a couple of hundred feet above them. All around were tumbled masses of weathered rock. It was a desolate, barren place. Without water, or vegetation. Nothing lived here, save for a few lizards and snakes.

Sung Shan watched with mild detachment as Ruger dismounted and began to move along the base of the rock wall. He clambered over, or crawled under boulders, his gaze fixed on the ground. He kept moving, searching, turning back and forth until he located himself. Sung Shan waited patiently, content to simply wait where he was. He was not used to so much riding and was feeling slightly uncomfortable. He endured his discomfort, ignoring the constant grumbling coming from the two men on the wagon. They were disagreeable men, he decided. No more than trash. He shared Ruger's views concerning the pair. The sooner they were out of the way the better he would feel. Shan would have favored the death of one of them to that of Brady, the man killed at the McAdam girl's cabin. Brady had been with Sung Shan and Chu. Though he had not been Chinese Shan had approved of him. Brady had been a dependable man – though not good enough at the end.

'Master Shan, he has found something,' Chu said. He spoke in his own tongue, never having been able to conquer English.

Shan gathered the reins of Ruger's horse, trailing it behind his own as he rode to where Ruger was waving a hand. Once he had attracted Shan the American went back to moving rocks from a pile.

'Chu, go and help him,' Shan ordered.

The large Chinese nodded. He stepped down from his horse and joined Ruger. Together they moved stone after stone until Shan was able to see a dark opening cutting into the rock face. Ruger straightened up, face glistening with sweat, grinning.

'What did I say?'

'I see only a black hole, Mister Ruger. Show me your gold and then I will have cause to be pleased.'

Ruger turned back to his work, a soft curse on his lips. *The hell with Shan.* He put his anger into his effort, throwing more rocks and stones aside. Chu worked silently beside him. They continued working until they had completely exposed the cave entrance. Bending low Ruger went inside, coughing at the dust swirling in the hot air. He allowed his eyes to adjust to the gloom before he went in too far. As he stepped over the rough ground he saw the stack of wooden crates. Long and narrow, layered with dust and earth. He still recognized them for what they were. He strode up to the stack and pushed the uppermost crate to the floor. The brittle, dry wood burst apart. Ruger bent down and closed a fist around one of the objects that had spilled from the crate. He lifted it, sensing its solid weight. Ruger turned and made his way back outside, walking up to Shan's horse.

'Convinced now, Mister Shan?'

He threw the object to the ground. It hit with a solid thud and lay gleaming in the sunlight.

It was a block of pure gold.

Sung Shan climbed down off his horse, bending to retrieve the gold block, examining it carefully. When he raised his head there was a thin smile on his lips. It was a cosmetic smile that did not reach his eyes.

'Mister Ruger, I do believe congratulations are in order.'

Ruger had moved to stand beside his horse. He took down his canteen and uncapped it. He splashed some water on his dusty face, then took a deep swallow.

'Shan, you're all heart.'

When he received no answer Ruger glanced up. Shan had already gone over to where Chu stood at the opening to the cave. The giant Chinese said something in his own tongue, to which Shan gave a brief reply.

'Something wrong?' Ruger asked, joining Shan.

'Chu has seen someone watching us. From that low ridge directly behind you. Do not look around. Let us allow him to believe he is safe. I would like to meet this man. We should bring out the gold and load it into the wagon. Leave our visitor to Chu.'

Six

Slumped in the scant shade of a huge boulder Brand wiped sweat from his face. He cursed the heat and the dust and the world in general. He was not in a particularly good mood. He had missed a lot of sleep the night before through the savage headache still throbbing inside his skull. At first light he had saddled up and moved on, still searching the trail he had lost the night before. It had taken him a good hour to locate it again, and shortly after he made the discovery that the man he was trailing was no longer alone. The tracks of two riders and a wagon joined up with the lone man. It had answered one of the questions floating around inside Brand's head. He had been wondering how the man named Ruger intended moving the gold if and when he found it. The wagon tracks explained that.

The second question had been answered soon after Brand had taken cover behind the boulder, and found he was able to watch Ruger and his four companions. Ruger had found the gold. Brand watched the men loading the long, narrow boxes into the wagon. The fact he had completed the first part of his assignment – locating Ruger and the gold – made little difference to Brand's mood. He still felt a deep-rooted anger at the price the gold had fetched. Too many people had already died. He wondered how many more would need to suffer before McCord decided to allow Brand to move in. The more he thought about McCord's desire to follow the gold to its final destination, the less he liked it. Not that it made any difference. Brand had his orders and as long as he was working for McCord he had to stay with them.

Brand eased away from the boulder, returning to where he had left his horse and reached for his canteen. It was already well over half empty. He splashed some on his face, rubbing the back of his neck with a wet hand. He allowed himself a small mouthful of the tepid water before hanging his canteen back on his saddle, then made his way back to his vantage point.

The wagon was still being loaded. There didn't seem to be any urgency in the way the men were working. Brand saw no problem with that. They had time on their side, and in the dry heat it was wiser to take things easy.

The minutes dragged by. Brand wondered how long he was going to have to hang around before Ruger and company moved out.

The faint sound behind him barely registered. Brand reacted instinctively, lunging off to one side and turning, his right hand snatching for the Colt on his hip. He was starting to rise, the revolver clear of his holster. He had already picked up the massive shape before him. Brand had a blurred glimpse of a brutal face, the head completely bald, gleaming in the bright sunlight. He saw too, the huge fist an instant before it clubbed him across the side of his head. Pain exploded inside his skull as Brand was knocked sideways. The impact stunned him. He skidded on his knees, the Colt slipping from his fingers. Trying to ignore the thundering pain in his head Brand struggled to regain his balance. His senses failed him and he saw too late the dark shape looming over him. He struck out, driving his fist at the wide body. It was like hitting a sandbag. He threw another punch, aiming for the face this time. A huge hand swatted his fist aside. A hard fist drove into his side, exploding breath from his body. Brand slumped to the ground, desperately sucking air into his starved lungs. He collapsed in the dust, feeling its sour taste in his mouth.

He lay motionless, his body burning with pain. His frustration was increased by his own weakness. He tried to climb to his feet. A hard boot lashed out and thudded against his side, spinning him over onto his back. Brand blinked against the blinding glare of the sun. A moment later the light was blocked by the towering form of his silent attacker. Hands reached down and grasped Brand's shirt. He felt himself being lifted off the ground as if he was a child in the powerful hands, The world spun before his eyes and then settled with jarring abruptness as he was thrown bodily across his own saddle, face down. His horse began to move, bouncing him roughly and Brand felt a raging sickness fill his throat. He wanted to get himself off the horse. Feel the hard ground under his feet so he could at least fight back. His spirit was willing but the flesh was weak, so he stayed where he was. A couple of times he blacked out. Each time it took longer to recover and he had the sense to resist an attempt at a premature come back.

The horse came to a halt. Brand caught the sound of voices. Men were speaking in hurried tones, one in particular in anger. Brand felt certain that anger was directed at him. Without warning hands caught hold of his clothing and he was thrown from the horse. He failed to break his fall and hit the ground on his left side, his face scraping the rough earth. He felt blood streak his jaw.

He was not allowed to lie for long. He was pulled into a sitting position, his back against a hard rock. Brand opened his eyes slowly, letting the spinning world settle. He stared up into five faces. Two of them were Chinese. One of the others he recognized as the man from the cabin. The one who had hit him.

'That's him. That's the son of a bitch. I should have killed him back at the cabin.'

Sung Shan allowed himself a shadowy smile. 'But you did not, Mister Ruger. Because of your failing we now have an added problem.'

Harvey Ruger straightened up. He put his hand to the butt of his revolver. 'I can soon put that to rights,' he said.

Sung Shan raised a slim hand. 'No, Mister Ruger. It is too late for that now.'

'What the hell you on about now, Shan?'

'Has it not occurred to you that this man may be from the law?'

Ruger laughed. 'You think that's going to stop me? Even lawdogs die when you shoot them.'

'Perhaps. But you agree with my thought?'

'So he's the law.' Ruger shook his head. 'Hell, I don't give a damn. Kill the bastard.'

'There are times, Mister Ruger, when I am in despair over you.'

'Meaning?'

'This man may have informed his superiors about us. He may have already passed along information to be used against us.'

'If he has learned anything, Shan, there ain't any way he could have passed it along. Not from out here.'

'I prefer caution, Mister Ruger. Until we know to the contrary we must assume the worst. It is in our interest to keep this man alive for now. Do not forget how much Master Han has invested in this venture. He does not tolerate mistakes. As you should know by now, Mister Ruger.'

Ruger scowled. He made no objections.

Sung Shan beckoned Chu. He took Brand's Colt from the big Chinese, then gave him swift instructions. He turned back to Brand.

'Until it has been decided what to do with you...*Mister...?*'

'The name is Brand.'

'So...as I was about to say, Brand, while there is the possibility you can furnish us with information you will be allowed to live. Do not presume that will remain permanent. You are of use only as long as our venture can be jeopardized.' Sung Shan paused, studying Brand silently for a moment. 'Just how much have you learned, Mister Brand?'

'I think I'll let you worry about that. Way I see it, Mister Shan, you're going to have plenty of time to do just that.'

Ruger lunged forward, his mouth taut. 'Give me ten minutes and I'll get your answers.'

'No chance, Ruger,' Brand said. You're out of your league. Killing old men and girls is the best you can do. You already missed your chance at me.'

'The hell you say!' Ruger smashed a boot into Brand's side. 'See how loud you crow after I kick the shit out of you.'

'Ruger. Leave him.' Sung Shan's tone was hard. Ruger stepped back, his expression betraying his feelings for the Chinese. 'I believe it will be better if you stayed away from Mister Brand. He will be well looked after by Chu.'

Brand glanced at the menacing, silent figure. Chu returned his scrutiny without a change of expression.

'You have already experienced Chu's talent for violence, Mister Brand,' Sung Shan said conversationally. 'He has vast and complicated skills at his command. It can be used to either caution someone, or to kill them. I am sure there is no need to say more.'

Shan turned away, Ruger following reluctantly. They moved to the wagon where the other two men waited. The loading commenced again as the long boxes from the cave were manhandled into the wagon.

Doing his best to ignore Chu's brooding bulk Brand leaned back against the rock. Like it or not, he had no say in any of the events about to take place. For once he was going to have to sit back and drift whichever way the wind blew. It had been his own fault Chu had overpowered him. But at least he was getting a close up view of what was happening, and perverse as it was, he had at least located the gold.

He watched them loading the boxes into the wagon. The gold in those boxes had a lot of people interested. McCord. Sung Shan. Ruger. Jenny McAdam had died because of it. Brand was interested in the gold too. It was the cause of his current predicament. One way or another he had to reverse that.

It took almost an hour to complete the loading, Sung Shan supervising the whole operation. It was only after the canvas sheet had been lashed down over the load that Shan returned to where Brand sat.

'We are ready to go now. Chu will bind your hands. Then you can climb on your horse. Chu will take your reins and lead you. Remember what I said earlier. Do not attempt to escape. I have told Chu that if you do he must stop you any way he can.'

'If he doesn't kill you, Brand, I will,' Ruger called as he mounted his own horse.

'I were you, Ruger, I'd be more concerned about keeping an eye on those gold bricks. Way things seem to be going you won't be keeping them long.'

'What the hell do you know?'

'Enough about that gold. And your friend Shan.'

'You're bluffin'.'

Brand didn't reply. It was easier to let Ruger worry. The more he had on his mind the less time he would have for baiting Brand. He needed to be able to concentrate on getting himself out of the trouble he was in. Getting Ruger off his back might allow him some breathing space. He was going to need it.

Seven

Muted sounds broke through the drug of sleep. Jason Brand roused himself, becoming aware of the ache that ran the length of his spine. He pushed into a sitting position, scrubbing a hand across his dry face. His fingers rasped against the thick beard stubble. The least they could have done was to have let him shave. He smiled at his own vanity. *What the hell did he need to shave for?* Right now he had no need for the niceties of life. A rising burst of anger brought him lurching to his feet and he stumbled around in semi-darkness until he tripped over a coil of rope. He went down on his knees, cursing his own weakness, and knew in the same instant that it was exactly what Sung Shan wanted. The Chinese had his own methods for breaking a man. Brand had already acknowledged the possible effectiveness of those methods.

He crawled on hands and knees until he reached the place where a small iron grille afforded him his only contact with the outside world. Pressing his face against it Brand stared out on a wide blue sky curving cleanly above a limitless spread of blue-green water. He felt the slight touch of a breeze against his skin and tasted the salt from the water that sprayed up from below the grille.

The Gulf of Mexico.

A wide and peaceful expanse of ocean that was a long way from the arid terrain of New Mexico. Brand narrowed his aching eyes against the bright gleam of the reflected sun and listened to the sounds around him. Sounds he had come to recognize over the past days. The soft flap of bleached sails catching the high winds and the constant creak of the tall masts flexing against the weight of canvas and rope. He could also hear the slap of the waves against the sides of the ship and the shrill cry of gulls as they wheeled and curved against the clean splash of the empty sky.

Somehow he had known what was waiting at the end of the two-day trip by train, taking them all the way out of New Mexico and through southern Texas. Sung Shan had the whole trip well organized. From the gold-cache they had traveled across country for three days, picking up a backwater spur line just below Gallup. The gold had been transferred into a freight car and stored in prepared wooden crates. A local cattle train had hooked them on in the late afternoon and just after midnight they had been shunted into a siding alongside the southbound tracks of the main Denver to El Paso route. In the early hours a long freight train had made a stop for water and when it moved on the freight car had been added to its complement. At El Paso they had left the Atchison, Topeka and Santa Fe line, joining the Southern Pacific. They traveled deep into Texas and completed their rail journey just below Corpus Christi. Sung Shan's pre-planning had been well worked out and another wagon and team had been waiting. The final stretch of their journey brought them to a quiet little bay along the coast from Port Isabel. On the evening tide Jason Brand got his first glimpse of the triple masted 250-foot clipper *The Gulf Queen*. The gold had been taken on board and stored in the after hold and before first light the ship raised anchor, turned about and had slipped quietly by Port Isabel, leaving behind the calm water of Laguna Madre. The thin spit of land known as Padre Island fell behind them in the early morning mist as *The Gulf Queen* set a southerly course out across the Gulf, the white yardarm pointing the way to Mexico.

For Jason Brand it meant being confined below decks, relieved only when he was brought a mug of water and a chunk of dry bread by one of the crewmen. On the second day the man himself put in an appearance, accompanied by the ever silent Chu. Sung Shan stood just inside the doorway, a thin smile playing around the corners of his mouth.

'I'll wager you were a bastard when you were a kid,' Brand said. He directed his words at Shan, but his gaze drifted beyond the man, taking in the open deck and the calm sea beyond. Nothing he saw offered much in the way of escape. Brand returned his gaze to Shan. 'I can just see you pulling the wings off flies.'

Sung Shan stared around Brand's cramped quarters. 'I hope you understand that I could not offer better accommodation, Brand,' he said. 'If it had been left to Mister Ruger you would already be dead and not enjoying the pleasure of a sea voyage.'

'I'm not so sure about it being good for my health.'

'That is of great concern to me,' Shan said. 'I am still undecided as to the extent of your knowledge over my affairs. As I said once before, you will be kept alive until the matter is determined one way or another. Once we reach our destination I will have ample time to devote to you.'

'The hell with you, Shan.'

Even now Brand could see the cold gleam in Sung Shan's eyes. Once the Chinese had him where he wanted, Brand's life would become decidedly uncomfortable. So he needed to do something to alter things. McCord's priorities didn't concern him any longer. It was down to pure survival – his own, and that took pride of place over everything else. If he managed to get himself free and clear of Shan and company, then he could follow up his assignment.

'We will talk again,' Shan had said.

He stepped back and the door thudded shut again.

Now peering through the grille Brand screwed his head round, trying to get a look towards the bow of the ship. At first all he could see was the blurred merging of sea and sky. He blinked against the bright glare, and as his eyes focused he made out a strip of tree-lined land. Below the trees was a pale beach, waves rolling against the sand. He realized then that the ship was turning in towards the land. He picked up the increasing activity on deck as the crew moved to man their stations.

He moved back from the grille and slumped against the bulkhead. Time was running out. The voyage was coming to an end. Probably at some rendezvous where Sung Shan would unload his gold. That meant Brand would be leaving the ship too. *But for where?* He didn't give it too much though. His main concern was his survival.

He stayed close to the grille, watching as the shoreline got closer. He saw they had entered a small bay and the beach was only a couple of hundred yards away. Close enough for Brand to see the wild growth of trees and undergrowth. The area looked uninhabited. First choice for an illegal landing of stolen gold.

He jerked away from the grille as he heard the bolt on the door being jerked back. He saw it swing open. Saw the stocky figure framed in the opening. One of the ship's crew.

'Come on, Yank, the Chinaman wants you on deck.' The voice was harsh. The accent British. The threat behind the tone was clear. To add emphasis to the order the revolver in the sailor's hand moved menacingly towards Brand's stomach. 'Buck up, Yank, or I'll let you have one your own bleedin' bullets.'

Brand stood up slowly, bracing himself against the bulkhead as the ship rolled slightly. He heard the man laugh softly. Brand crossed to the door, ignoring the gun. He had already noticed it was his own Colt. That angered him more than anything else. The bastards were already dividing up his belongings.

'Blimey, I thought you cowboys were fast on your feet.'

As Brand drew level with the door the sailor stepped aside but reached out an impatient hand to push him out onto the deck. The moment was ill chosen. A sudden swell rolled the ship and the sailor was forced to shift his stance as the deck canted. For a second the Colt's barrel moved away from Brand and he took the chance, pushing from the door, driving his shoulder into the crewman's chest. His right hand reached out, finger's closing over the Colt's hammer. Brand slammed the point of his left elbow into the sailor's exposed stomach. The man grunted, winded, eyes staring wildly as he struggled against Brand's weight. Aware he didn't have the strength for a prolonged struggle Brand hauled himself around and kneed the sailor savagely in the groin. As the man sagged Brand slammed his left hand under the sailor's chin and rammed his head back against the solid door frame. All resistance went and as the man sagged Brand snatched his Colt free, turning to step out on deck.

And found himself lost in a world of tall masts and flapping canvas, ropes and rigging. A world where the deck moved under his feet. The sudden cold splash of spray rising over the ship's side snapped him back to some degree of normality. He felt the ship roll and threw out a hand to hang on to a rope, eyes searching the way ahead.

He heard a shout. Brand spun, saw a moving figure, and ducked as he spotted the raised revolver in the man's hand. He heard the vicious crack of the weapon. The bullet chunked into the wood railing only feet away, raising splinters. A second shot smacked against the wind, this bullet tugging at Brand's shirt sleeve. He lunged forward, crouching and snapped off a quick shot. He knew he had missed even as he fired but at least the closeness made the other man draw back. Brand saw him bobbing up and down, using deck clutter for cover. He waited, taking his time, and fired again when he felt satisfied. This time he made a hit and the target twisted as blood and fragments of cloth burst from his shoulder. The hit man stumbled, losing his revolver as he went down on his knees. Brand saw his own exposed position as close to being suicidal. Attack could – and would – come from any number of directions. He had no offensive advantages, or defensive ones. At most he had four shots left. After that...

In the seconds his enemies organized themselves Brand assessed his position, weighed his options – he changed that to a single option – and took it.

He jammed the Colt down behind his belt, turned and ran for the side of the ship. In the instant before he went over the side he looked down at the blue-green water, figuring he was way out of his depth in more ways than one, then he was falling.

As he cleared the rail a shot rang out, the bullet ripping a furrow across the top of his left shoulder. The pain made him yell and he barely managed to suck in air before he hit the water and sank below the surface. He fought against rising too quickly, aware he needed to gain some distance from the ship. He kicked out with his legs, driving himself through the water until his starving lungs demanded he offer them air. Bubbles streamed from his lips as he pushed towards the surface. The sun blinded him for a moment as his head cleared the water. Gasping wildly Brand made vain attempts to steady himself against the pull of the current. He looked out for the shore but found the ship first. *The Gulf Queen*, already yards away, still loomed large. Brand was still able to make out Ruger and Sung Shan at the stern rail. There were others too. Members of the crew. Armed. They had rifles and they started to fire. Brand heard the whip crack of the shots. Bullets zipped angrily through the water around him, but it was hard for the shooters to make accurate fire due to the roll of the ship.

Brand felt a sudden, powerful force grip him. He was lifted and hurled shoreward by the swell of the water. The power of the waves proved too much for him. Brand was overwhelmed, flung back and forth. In the end he went with the flow, realizing he couldn't do a thing to prevent it. He concentrated on keeping his head above water, snatching in air whenever he could. He kept getting brief glimpses of the green shoreline as he was turned and twisted by the current, his battered body aching. He swallowed mouthfuls of water, choking and gasping as the waves slammed him down, then lifted him in a terrifying moment before dropping him yet again. The action was repeated over and over. He was lost in an alien environment, the pressure from tons of water forcing him down until he was dragged along the sandy seabed. Gravel and sand tore at his flesh and clothes. His senses dulled. He was barely aware of being flung into shallow water, rolled back and forth by the crashing waves until they reluctantly retreated and left him sprawled on the beach.

Brand lay motionless. He could still hear the rolling sound of the waves close by, the water still tugging at his legs. He was still not fully aware of his surroundings. It was only when his stomach rejected the salt water he had swallowed, making him retch violently, that he finally realized where he was. When his retching ceased he lay shivering despite the hot sun. It took him some time before he recovered enough to be able to drag himself to his knees and crawl up the dry, sandy beach until he reached the fringe of palm trees. He lay on the warm sand and passed out.

Eight

He opened his eyes to a night sky bright with stars. Brand could smell the heady scent of flowers. The warm air held the salty tang of the sea and he picked up the soft rush of waves close by. He recalled his desperate struggle in those same waves. A time he had almost given himself little chance of survival. But he *had* survived. And that was all that mattered.

Brand sat up, reaching for the Colt he had pushed behind his belt. It wasn't there. And something else was out of place. He remembered dragging himself up off the beach and hiding in the deep undergrowth. Now he was sitting on blanket, in a small clearing.

What the hell was going on?

He pushed to his feet and felt the world spin around him. He was still weak. His body was stiff, aching, and he could feel the raw gash across his shoulder where the stray bullet had caught him.

A soft sound reached his ears. Brand turned, eyes searching he gloom. He made out a shadowed figure, standing motionless. Then a soft laugh. A gentle, almost musical sound.

'So, you wake up at last, *hombre*.' The voice was female, young. The accent unmistakably Mexican, softening the English. 'I thought you would sleep all night.'

'I still might.'

The figure moved closer. He saw a supple, gently curved body clad in a simple cotton dress. The girl's brown skin gleamed softly in the moonlight as she came to stand in front of him, hands resting on her hips. She stared at him, her large brown eyes constantly on the move. Even in the poor light Brand could see she was beautiful.

'You are American?'

'So they tell me.' Brand turned to look around. Yards away he saw a small hut. 'Where am I?'

The girl smiled, showing her white teeth. 'You do not know?' She laughed gently. 'Are you lost, *hombre*?'

'Damn right.'

'This place is called the Bay of Caves. Along the coast is Agua Verde.'

'This is Yucatan? Mexico?'

'Of course.' The girl paused, frowning. 'You *are* lost, *hombre*.'

He shrugged. 'Hey, you got my gun?'

'*Si*. It is inside the hut. You want it?'

'I'd feel safer with it in my hand. Listen do you have any food? I can't pay you anything right now but...'

'I have food. I do not ask for money.'

He caught the defensive tone in her voice.

'Sorry. I don't mean to offend you.'

She nodded and Brand followed her to the hut.

'Why did you jump from the ship?' she asked as they entered the hut.

'You saw?'

'*Si*. Why were you on *The Gulf Queen*? It is a bad ship.'

'You know of it?'

She lit a lamp, the glow exposing the neat interior of the hut.

'A bad ship,' she repeated. 'It belongs to Mister Han. He also is very bad.'

'You've heard of Han?'

'I know of him. And the people who work for him. Bad *hombres*.' As she spoke she was feeding wood into a small stove that stood in a corner of the hut. She placed a blackened pot over the flames. Moving to a shelf she picked up plates and spoons and placed them on a small table under the hut's open window. 'You have trouble with those men?'

'I will if they catch me.'

She indicated for him to sit, then brought him cheese and a chunk of coarse bread. When the pot on the stove began to steam she brought cups and poured out rich, dark coffee. It was a basic meal, but Brand ate with a good appetite. The coffee was especially good. It had a pleasant flavor he wasn't used to.

He watched the girl as she moved around the hut. She looked extremely capable. Independent and proud of her ability to survive on her own. When she came to pour him more coffee she smiled in a free and easy way.

'What do I call you?' he asked.

'My name is Angelina,' she said. A warm laugh passed her lips and she ran a hand through the thick mane of black hair. 'No one calls me that now. Not since I was small. Everyone calls me Angel.'

Brand drained his coffee. 'Well, that's what you've been to me.'

'You have a name too?'

'Jason Brand.'

'Welcome to Mexico, Jason Brand.'

After she had cleared the table Angel brought him his Colt. She sat across from him and watched as Brand stripped the gun down, wiping it carefully with a dry rag she had provided. He was able to clean the gun – but he had concerns over the bullets. If seawater had got in at the powder...

'You mind if I rest up a while?'

Angel shook her head. 'As long as you need.'

'I need to get into town soon as possible.'

'To do with Han?'

Brand nodded. 'Angel, I don't want you to get involved. Once that ship makes port Shan will have his boys out looking for me. They turn up here it could mean trouble for you.'

'Since I was old enough to know what the word means trouble has never been far away. *Hombre,* do not worry about Angel.'

'I'm not letting...'

'Brand, I ask you a question. Do you know how to get into Agua Verde without being seen?' She flicked a long finger at him. 'Angel does.'

'You always argue about everything?'

'*Si.*'

Brand felt his eyes closing. He was having difficulty staying awake. Tiredness washed over him and like it or not he knew he needed some sleep. He had taken a beating from jumping ship and battling the current. He felt the heavy Colt sag in his grip, the barrel hitting the table.

'Come, *hombre,* it is time to rest.'

He heard Angel's voice from a long way off. Then he felt her strong hands helping him to stand, moving him away from the table and across the hut. He didn't resist. He hadn't the will left in him. If Sung Shan and his people came now...it didn't matter at all...

Angel woke him as the first flood of sunlight brightened the hut's interior. She had managed to get him to the low bed that was pushed against one wall, covering him with a couple of blankets and he had slept through the night without waking once. Now she waved a mug of coffee under nose, the rich aroma working wonders on his senses. He sat up and drank the hot brew.

'Tell me who you are, Brand,' Angel asked suddenly.

'Who do you think I am?'

She took a long look at him. Despite his ragged, unshaven appearance, she recognized something in him that confirmed her earlier thoughts when he had sat cleaning the Colt. She had watched the way he had concentrated on the weapon, its ability to work uppermost in his mind.

'I think you are a *pistolero*.'

'You know many *pistoleros*?'

'Enough to recognize the breed.'

He drained the coffee and pushed to his feet, swaying a little until he got his balance. He moved around the hut a while, easing the stiffness from his body. Then he crossed to the table where his gun lay. He picked it up and thumbed in the bullets with little enthusiasm. His priority was a supply of fresh ammunition. A greater one was staying alive long enough to get his hands on that ammunition.

'Angel, I'd feel happier if you just pointed me towards Agua Verde and left me to it.'

'I am going there any way. For my work.'

He recognized the stubborn look in her eyes and realized there was no way he was going to get the better of this young woman. Resigned, he cleaned up and as soon as Angel was ready they left the hut. She led the way with the casual ease of someone who knew the area well. As they moved through trees and thick, lush undergrowth, with no visible path in sight. Brand followed her, ever cautious, his hand resting on the Colt tucked in his belt. After a good hour they broke out of the trees and found themselves presented with open, untouched terrain. Now a narrow, dusty trail wound its way between stretches of grass. Brand touched her arm as she made to walk on.

'This trail lead anywhere?'

'Only to a small village.'

'Better if we went round,' he said. 'Villages mean people and people can mean trouble.'

'Brand, you are a very suspicious *hombre*.'

He smiled at her. 'It's the reason I've stayed alive for so long. Don't take anything on trust.'

'You trust me?'

'Man'd be a fool not to trust an angel.'

She laughed, her brown eyes sparkling. 'I think you have a very smooth tongue, Jason Brand.'

They had moved no more a few yards the sound of pounding hooves reached their ears. Brand turned and saw four mounted men coming over a rise, sunlight glinting on gun metal as they spotted Brand and Angel. Dust rose in the wake of the thundering horses as they bore down on the exposed pair.

'Angel, back under cover,' he yelled, grabbing her wrist and hauling along behind him as they sought to return to the cover of the trees and undergrowth they had only recently cleared.

The clatter of hooves increased. Brand heard a man yell, the shout was followed by the flat, harsh sound of a handgun firing. The bullet kicked up dirt feet ahead of Brand. He increased his pace, hearing Angel gasp as she struggled to stay upright. More shots came, but the shooters were firing from the backs of galloping horses and their aim was way off. Then they were into the undergrowth, keen shrubbery whiplashing their bodies. Neither hesitated, ignoring the sting of the greenery. More shots sounded, the bullets clipping leaves and shredding bark from the trunks of trees.

Any hope the dense shrubbery might halt their pursuers was dashed when the lead rider drove his horse forward. He yelled and cursed the animal, digging in his heels to force it on. His arm ached from yanking on the rein and he struck at the horse's flank with the barrel of his revolver. As he rode through the shadowed timber, his keen eyes searched for his quarry. He saw nothing. There was no sound or movement other than his own. Then he began to catch glimpses of his three companions as they rode deeper into the timber. They were all aware of the price of failure. They had been searching since first light, looking for the American who had escaped from Sung Shan. Master Han's anger had been terrible to see and it had only been due to Sung Shan's excellent record of service that had prevented Han from taking out his anger on his second in command. Master Han was widely known for his lack of patience with those who let him down. He had no compunction in using the most severe penalty if one of his people failed him. The four riders were all aware of what would happen to them if they did not return with the American.

The first rider reined in his horse and sat motionless in his saddle, listening closely, eyes moving back and forth. Here in this shadowed place there was too much to draw the eye with false promises. There were too many moving patches of dark and light where the sun lanced down through the greenery. The rider reached a decision and slid from the saddle, his revolver cocked and ready in his hand. He moved forward, peering into the greenery, pausing here and listening, hoping he might find what he was looking for. Nothing. It was as if the American and the girl had vanished. The man straightened, irritation marking his face. He knew Brand could not be that far ahead. He had only been yards behind them and they would have to move quietly too, so they were still close.

A flash of movement caught his attention. It was off to his left side. The flicker vanished just as swiftly as it had shown and the man decided it must have been a trick of the light. Almost in the same breath he realized his mistake but by then it was far too late.

Jason Brand rose from the ground without a sound. He swung the heavy Colt in a short, brutal arc, catching the man just above the left ear. The man grunted once, falling to his knees and Brand hit him a second time, a solid blow that laid the man face down on the ground.

'Angel, take hold of that damn horse,' Brand snapped as he crouched beside the man. He loosened the belt and holster from the man's waist. He quickly buckled it around his own waist. Then he picked up the gun the man had dropped. It was a .44 Smith &

Wesson. He ejected the spent cartridges and replaced them from the loads in the belt loops. He jammed his own Colt in behind the belt.

'Know him?' Brand asked Angel as she led the horse up close.

She nodded. 'One of Han's Chinese.'

Brand hauled himself into the saddle, reaching down to drag Angel up behind him. She sat close, her arms around his body. At any other time it would have been something to enjoy. Right now Brand's thoughts were far away from any kind of pleasure.

'Hold on,' he said and gigged the horse forward, pushing it on through the greenery. The animal wasn't too happy with all the shrubbery lashing against it and Brand had to keep it on a short rein as it tried to protest. 'Damn you, horse, quit playing foolish. This isn't a Sunday walk we're on.'

He wanted – needed – to gain distance between himself and Han's men. There were three more of them in the vicinity and every one would be out to take his scalp – or whatever the Chinese equivalent was. Brand had no intention of finding out.

A dark shape burst out of the greenery ahead. Another of Han's riders. The man was trying to control his horse and take a shot at Brand at the same time. It caused a delay and it was that delay that Brand took advantage of. He hauled in his own mount, the horse squealing against the pressure of the bit in its mouth. Brand leaned across the horse's arched neck, leveling his own revolver, not firing until he had his target. He squeezed the trigger and heard the Smith &

Wesson thump out its shot. The heavy gun kicked back in his hand. The bullet took the Chinese in the chest, twisting him in his saddle. Brand had his range now and he fired a second time, this time driving the man off his horse and slamming him face down on the ground.

Yanking his skittish horse back under control Brand moved it forward, aware that the shots would alert the other two riders.

'*Which way, damnit?*' he snapped.

Angel jabbed a finger ahead of them, 'That way, and don't be angry with me. I haven't shot at you.' There was a pointed silence before she added, '*Yet.*'

Brand smiled at that. He kicked hard against the horse's sides. The animal decided it had suffered enough and took off at a hard pace, weaving in and out of the trees and shrubbery. As their pace increased Brand thought they might yet outrun Han's men. Then fate decided otherwise and the horse rose beneath him as it tried to clear a half-concealed, rotting tree that had fallen long ago. One of its forelegs caught against the decayed trunk and it fell, shrilling loudly. As it began to go down Brand twisted and made a grab for Angel, dragging her from the horse. As they hit the mossy ground they rolled away from the horse as it crashed down only feet away. Thrashing hooves missed them by inches. The horse, snorting in terror, rolled and regained its feet. Before Brand, winded by the fall, could gain his own feet the horse had galloped off into the distance and out of reach.

Brand hauled Angel up beside him.

'You still sure you did the right thing sticking with me?'

Before she could make any reply a gun exploded close by. The bullet hit a tree, filling the air with white splinters of sap-moist wood. A second bullet clipped the skirt of Angel's dress. Brand took her hand and they moved quickly, heading for the densest part of the timber. Brand could hear shouting behind them, the noise of clumsy pursuit. Han's men were down to two and they would be getting ever more anxious to complete the job they had been sent to do.

They broke into a clearing. Brand spotted the gleam of water at the bottom of a hollow. He caught Angel's shoulders and spun her round to face him.

'This time no questions,' he said, pulling her to the rim of the hollow. 'Just get down there and stay under cover. Don't move. Don't talk. I need to be on my own for this. *Go.*'

She did as she was told, sliding down the side of the hollow and concealed herself in the thick mess of foliage at the bottom, trying and failing to stay out of the water.

Brand turned away from the hollow, stepping back into the thick greenery, reloading the .44 as he went. He had a killing job to do and the only way was to do it fast, giving his opponents no chance to hit back. It was the kind of work Brand was suited to. A part of him he wasn't overly proud of, but when he was put in harm's way he had no hesitation in allowing that side of his character to take over.

He located the two Han men. They were on foot, leading their horse as they searched the shrubbery. They were both armed, moving quietly as they advanced. They both snapped around when Brand stepped into the open, his revolver already moving to his first target. He shot the taller of the pair first, putting a single bullet through his head. The Chinese had time for a shocked grunt before he hit the ground. His partner was slightly more agile and as Brand shifted his aim, this one threw himself flat. The revolver in his hand made a flat sound, powder smoke lashing from the muzzle. The bullet cleaved empty air. Brand had changed position the moment he fired his first shot. As the hammer fell on the Chinese shooter's gun Brand was already crouching, his own weapon lining up. He fired twice, placing the .44 slugs into the Chinese as the man started to rise. The heavy impact kicked the Chinese over and he died staring up at the sky.

Brand took time to gather the reins of the horses the Chinese had left some way back. He led them back to where he had left Angel and told her she could come out from cover. There was a long silence before she finally appeared, shaking water from her skirt. She stood in front of him, refusing to meet his gaze.

'Hell of a way to start the day,' he said lamely, then added, 'Angel, I'm sorry I got you mixed up in all this.'

'Never have I had guns fired at me before. It frightened me.'

'How do you think I feel?'

Now she looked at him. 'You were frightened too?'

'Believe it, Angel. The day I go through something like this without getting scared is the day I retire.'

'Is that supposed to make me feel better?'

Brand had to smile at that. 'Hell, I don't know.' He handed her the reins of one of the horses. 'Let's just get out of here.'

They mounted up and Angel rode ahead, Brand trailing her. He tried to relax but found it hard. The realization that Han seemed determined to bury him in Mexico didn't settle well. The man had his people looking for Brand and with a great deal of animosity in their actions. Going to Agua Verde did not appear to hold out much in the way of comfort for Brand with Han's men on the prod. Whatever the Chinese planned to do with the gold shipment, it was big enough for him to want Brand out of the picture.

And now that the Chinese had shown his hand Brand was more determined than ever to get to the bottom of the mystery surrounding the stolen gold. Perhaps when he arrived in Agua Verde he might be able to find answers to the questions crowding his mind.

Nine

They reached Agua Verde mid-morning. The port town, built around the harbor and running back into low hills, was a noisy place. Angel brought them in through the outskirts, keeping to isolated side streets until she halted at the side of a warehouse off the harbor. She slid off the horse and handed the reins to Brand.

'I will walk from here to the cantina where I work. It would look strange if I arrived on a horse If you come looking for me it is easy to find on the harbor front. You remember my directions?'

Brand nodded. He dismounted and went to where she stood. He took her arm and pulled her close, kissing her quickly, feeling the easy press of her body against his.

'You be careful,' he said.

'Angel is always careful. *Hombre*, I will be all right. You watch out for Han and his men.'

He nodded. 'Thanks for your help, Angel. If things go right I may come looking for you.'

'I would like that, Jason Brand,' she said.

He watched her go. He did hope he might get a chance to see her again, but knowing the way his life ran that might not happen, and right now he had enough to keep him busy.

He led the pair of horses down a side alley and tethered them to a fence post. If someone didn't steal them he might have a ride when he got back. He had decided against riding into Agua Verde on horses he had taken from Han's men because they might be recognized. He was going to have to go in on foot, playing it by ear until he got a line on Han and his base. He figured it wouldn't be too hard. There couldn't be that many Chinese in the Mexican town of Agua Verde.

As it turned out it took Brand very little time to make contact with Han's men. And oddly it was not with his Chinese. It happened very quickly, not the way he had expected, nor wanted, but he had no say in the matter. He was making his way through the maze of back streets, heading in the general direction of the harbor when he gained company.

He didn't see the man until it was too late. A tall figure moved up alongside him and Brand felt something hard jab into his left side. He glanced around and looked into the hard face a lean man clad in a tan colored suit. Pale, cold eyes regarded Brand with unconcealed hostility.

'Turn into this alley, Brand,' Hardface said. He added force to his order by increasing the pressure of the gun barrel in Brand's side. 'Walk naturally, mate.'

The British accent confirmed Brand's familiarity with the man's face. He had been on board *The Gulf Queen*. It looked like Han had his people already covering the streets of Agua Verde.

As they entered the alley another man stepped into view. He was sandy haired, his bony face pale and pockmarked.

'Seems you have been something of a bastard,' Hardface said. He glanced at his partner and smiled. 'Mister Han takes it personal like when you go round shooting his boys. He's a very aggressive Chinaman. Hates interference in his business. So that means you are in big trouble.' Hardface moved round so he was facing Brand. 'Sammy, take matey's guns before he gets any ideas. These bloody Yanks are all trigger happy.'

Sammy leaned across and slid Brand's Colt from his belt, fingers groping for the butt of the holstered Smith & Wesson. For a fraction of a second his shoulder moved between Brand and Hardface. Brand lunged forward, catching Sammy in the chest. Pushing hard he drove Sammy bodily into Hardface and in the confusion of them trying to separate Brand snatched the Smith & Wesson from its holster. He lashed out, the heavy barrel clouting Sammy under the jaw, putting everything he had into the brutal blow. Bone crunched. Sammy gave a scream of agony. Brand pushed by him, ignoring the threat of Hardface's own revolver. He thrust forward and up, hearing Hardface's weapon explode with sound. Then he was on the man, ramming his knee into Hardface's groin, ripping a howl of pain from the man. Coming to his full height Brand swung a bunched left and punched the man across the chin, spinning him round. Hardface hit the wall, bounced off and walked directly into the glittering arc of metal as Brand struck out with the Smith & Wesson again. He caught Hardface across the side of the skull, pitching the man face down on the street. A flurry of movement in the corner of his eye brought him face to face with the injured Sammy. His left hand was clamped around his shattered, bleeding jaw, his right fumbling under his jacket for his own holstered revolver. For a moment they eyed each other, then Sammy, despite being caught unready, continued to drag his weapon free, tearing the lining of his jacket in the process. As the weapon began its move to line up on him Brand leveled the .44 and put two bullets into Sammy's body. At close range the slugs blew out close to Sammy's backbone. He gave a choked cry as he was tumbled to the ground in a bloody heap...and even as Sammy was falling Brand heard gunfire. One bullet missed, the second burned across his right side. The shots had come from Hardface, on his knees by the wall, one hand pressed against the adobe to support himself, his bloody face twisted in a scowl of anger as he tried for a third shot. He failed to make it. Brand fired first, his shots precise and unhurried. He placed his .44 slugs in Hardface's chest, directly over the heart, kicking the tall man backwards. Hardface hit the ground, body arching like a drawn bow in response to the impact of the bullets. He held himself in that position for long seconds before he dropped to the ground and finally lay still.

Brand leaned against the wall. He felt weary and more than a little sick. The bullet graze burned his side. He was trembling, reaction to the sudden violent outburst and despite the hot sun he felt cold. He was also becoming angry. A slow mood of resentment towards the faceless man who seemed almost fanatical in his determination to Brand killed. He had only been on Mexican soil for a short time yet he had been forced to spend most of it running for his life and killing to hang on to it. He had a feeling too, that it wasn't about to end yet.

He became aware of a babble of voices. When he looked round the end of the ally was blocked by a gaping and noisy crowd of onlookers. At least there was one thing that was the same everywhere he went. The ability of violence and death to gather a crowd. They came to look, to stare, to absorb the sight and the smell of death.

Over the buzz of the crowd Brand heard louder, harsher voices. Snapping out orders. He picked out the odd word and phrase in Spanish. He also caught a sight of uniformed figures pushing through the throng.

Gray uniforms.

The Rurales.

The Mexican law force. Not always Brand's favorite people. He'd had run ins with them before and not always cordial meetings.

Brand let the Smith & Wesson slip from his fingers. Then he did the same with his Colt. He kicked both weapons away and stood passive, offering no resistance when the three armed, gray uniformed Mexicans broke through the crowd to confront him.

They surveyed the scene, discussing the implications between themselves. Brand remained where he was. No point in attracting more trouble.

Rifles were pointed at him. The man in charge, a burly Sergeant, waved a pistol at Brand.

'You will come with us,' he said. His English was clear, but heavily accented. 'This matter is to be resolved. Until then you will be locked up. You understand?'

'Yes.'

There was little else he could do at this point in time.

He was escorted through the crowd and along the streets of Agua Verde, and half an hour later he was locked in a cell at the Rurales headquarters.

His time in the cell became swiftly uncomfortable. The sergeant who had escorted him there seemed to have an aversion to *gringo* prisoners. Brand found himself wondering who had upset the man and what they had done to create such animosity.

When the door was opened to the cell the Sergeant, a large, scowling figure wearing a drooping

Zapata moustache started to grin. He handed the ring of keys to one of the other men then turned, without warning and caught Brand off-guard. Heavy hands grabbed Brand's clothing and he was hurled bodily into the cell, unable to stop himself from slamming into the stone wall on the other side. The Sergeant followed him in, to cries of encouragement from his men and started to pummel Brand in the body. He was muttering ceaselessly.

Brand was about to fight back when caution stayed his hand. He realized this was exactly what the Sergeant wanted him to do. One blow from Brand, witnessed by the other Rurales, would back up the Sergeant's claim that he had been attacked and was merely defending himself. So despite his desire to return the favor Brand covered his body as well as he could and took his punishment. It lasted until the Mexican had exhausted his rage and stood back, breathing heavily, still muttering and angry because the *gringo* had refused to take the bait. He walked out of the cell, slamming the door and locking it.

Brand slumped down on the edge of the crude, filthy cot, his arms wrapped around his bruised and aching body. He gingerly sucked air into his lungs, feeling the strain the action placed on his sore ribs. Movement caught his eye and he looked across at the cell door. There was a viewing slit set in the door and he could see a pair of eyes studying him. He knew it was the Sergeant, sizing up his victim, most probably for the next session. Brand stared the man out. The slit was closed with a bang.

Brand leaned back against the grubby wall, feeling the chill of the cold stone through his shirt. There was a barred window high over his head and he could hear the sounds of the street beyond. Normal sounds. Voices raised in conversation. The sudden sweet sound of a young woman's laughter. He smiled, wondering what, or who, had given her such pleasure.

So, he thought, *this is your world turning about and kicking you in the teeth.*

He knew that sooner or later he would get out of this situation. He always did. The hard times were expected in his line of work, and he would have been a damn fool not to expect them to occur. The only thing was that just lately he seemed to be getting his own and everyone else's share. He wondered how long his body could go on accepting this harsh treatment. When would it just curl up and quit on him? Jason Brand didn't consider himself an indestructible individual. He had proved that the many times he had bled over the years. Bullets and knives had all taken their toll, and he saw a future where one day, some day, that special bullet would wing its way towards him – and for once his luck would desert him and it would all be over.

Any man, whether he admitted it or not, liked to feel he was immortal. That he would go on forever, untouched by age, or frailty, or simple illness. Those things only happened to other people. Not to himself. Somehow he would keep on going, shrugging off the specter of death. It was a dream, nothing more than a fantasy conjured up in the mind of the young when they really did believe life was never ending. That time when old age and death was so far away it didn't register.

Jason Brand had known sudden death and the pain of loss at an early age. That had been when his family had been wiped out by a roving band of Kwahadi Comanche on a murder raid out from Texas, who had crossed into New Mexico and had come across the ranch where the Brand family lived. In the ensuing melee Jason Brand's father and mother had been slaughtered. His sister had been taken captive by the leader of the band, and later during her captivity had been murdered by the same warrior, Three Finger.

Brand had been the only survivor.

He had stayed alive because of a burning need for vengeance against the Comanche and the three white ranch hands who had run out and left his family to fend for themselves.

Two days before the massacre that made the boy shed his youth and become a man full grown, Jason Brand had celebrated his 18th birthday.

Those fiery days and the weeks that followed had formed his character, and his eventual survival had burned within him until it turned him like treated steel. He learned early in life about the whispers of betrayal, the need for self dependency and caution in everything. He had learned hard and fast, taking heed of the lessons, and using them to guide his adult life. He understood pain and he accepted it. He took his pleasures when they offered themselves, the same as food and water, always aware he might be denied any or all of them at any time.

It might have turned him into a walking dead man, cold and without feelings. He often maintained a grim exterior, when it suited his purpose, but there was a man of warmth and loyalty inside the tough veneer. Those who knew him well would have trusted themselves on his word alone, because he was a man of honor – a trait that some might find hard to accept. Brand did not outwardly display his emotions because he felt he had no need to. He owed nothing to any man, unless that man proved himself worthy, and then he would have ridden a thousand miles to offer his help to that person.

He came into his world of violence and pain because fate seemed determined to make him tread that path. He had tried on more than one occasion to remove himself from it, but each time events drew him back. In time he realized there was no escape. His fast gun. His predilection towards the violent land he walked had been hard earned and came with a price. It was a curse that cloaked him like a black shroud. He could never escape it. He bent to its demands and looked to his future with the clear eyed gaze of someone who saw, understood and fully accepted his destiny.

And there were not many who could say that.

The *Rurales* Sergeant knew nothing of this, and that was why when he looked at the gaunt face of his *gringo* prisoner he saw only the enemy. One who had to be defeated. He was mistaken. No matter what he did to

Brand he would never, ever, defeat him. Jason Brand understood his life and the manner in which it ran, so he was able to take anything the Sergeant threw his way and swallow it whole.

In the next two hours the Sergeant came to the cell three more times.

Each time he did his best to humiliate his prisoner. To make him suffer in the hope he would strike back. Each time he failed and that made him angrier. On the third visit he brought with him a short black leather whip. He had used the whip many times and it had never let him down. Men who sank to their knees with the bloody flesh of their bodies hanging in livid strips, were very prone to capitulation. Brand simply stood and faced his tormentor, hands at his sides as the Sergeant slashed the gleaming whip back and forth, each time getting closer. He was about to administer the first lash when a hard voice cut through the silence of the cell.

'Explain what exactly is going on here, Sergeant. Tell me because I would like to hear your excuses for this outrage.'

The Sergeant turned to see the immaculately uniformed figure of his commander. The young Major, who had only been transferred to Agua Verde a short while ago, was standing in the door of the cell. Calm and poised, he waited while the Sergeant tried to come up with a good excuse.

'I thought not,' the Major said. 'I was told when I came here to watch out for your treatment of prisoners. Why this unit had the worst record for deaths among them. Now I can see for myself. I have been watching you for a while, gathering my evidence. Today you have given me what I need to complete my investigation.'

The Major stepped into the cell. He took the whip from the hand of the Sergeant, studying it carefully before handing it to his own Sergeant.

'In the morning, *private*, you will be transferred to the interior division. You will report to Major Uvalde, who I understand, is even stricter than I could ever hope to be. He runs a very disciplined troop patrolling the western mountain territory. If I ever see your face in Agua Verde again, this matter will be brought to the attention of the disciplinary division and I will make it my personal business to see you pay the fullest price for your transgressions. Now get out of my sight.'

The Major waited until they were alone before he turned to Brand.

'Whatever your crime, this was unwarranted. Please accept my apologies. I will return later and we will discuss your case.'

He turned and left, the cell door closing behind him. Brand stood and stared at it for a while, then sat down on the edge of the cot, shaking his head at the sudden turn of events.

One minute he was getting himself ready for a hard time. The next a Major of the Rurales was apologizing for the treatment he had received.

What next?

A full pardon and the freedom of Agua Verde?

In the event Brand wasn't far off. He didn't get the freedom of the town — but a complete stranger showed up and got his release from the jail.

Ten

'I will ask one more time, *senor*. What is your business in Mexico? And especially Agua Verde? More importantly why did you kill those men?'

'You mean the ones who were doing their best to kill me?' Brand leaned forward on the edge of the low cot. 'Or has that been conveniently forgotten?'

The uniformed officer considered what Brand had just said.

'I have only your word you acted in self defence. The dead cannot make their story known. You understand this places the burden of proof on yourself. And I know nothing about you except you are a stranger in Agua Verde. Put yourself in my position, senor. What would you do?'

Brand had to give the man that one. He wasn't about to push his luck with this one. He was unusually polite for a member of the *Rurales*. The Mexican law force had a reputation that went before it. They were known to be tough, often ruthless, and their attitude was one of indifference to anyone brought before them, especially *gringos* This Major Ruiz, young and correct in his manner, was different, and Brand had no intention of making him angry. Ruiz had already proved his worth by stopping Brand from receiving a savage whipping from the cell block Sergeant. That had gone a long way towards convincing him all *Rurales* officers were not the same.

It had been nothing more than bad luck that had involved Brand with the two hardcases working for Han, and a continuation of the same black streak delivering him into the hands of the *Rurales*. It was as if he had been dealt bad cards from the start of the game. Nothing had gone right for him. Brand was used to setbacks but he'd had more than his fair share this time out. Maybe he was getting soft. Losing his edge. He shook away the thoughts. Allowing himself to wallow in self-pity was not his way. He was still on form. Tired perhaps from all that had happened. And now this endless questioning from a man young enough to be fresh from training school.

Brand sighed, reining in his feelings, and did what he could to answer the Major's questions without giving too much away.

Later, alone in his dingy cell, he lay staring up at the sunlight streaming through the bars of the window.

Dust motes floated lazily in the yellow shafts. Black flies buzzed in and out of the window. His presence attracted them and Brand swatted them away impatiently. He sat up, running a hand through his thick hair. He slid his hands down across his face, feeling the rough whiskers there. He needed a shave. And a bath, then a change of clothing. He wasn't going to place any bets when that might happen.

He pushed to his feet and began to pace the cell, using the movement to ease the stiffness from his body. He was still walking back and forth when he heard footsteps approaching the cell. He heard voices too, one the unmistakable Spanish accented English of Major Ruiz. A bolt was snapped back and the heavy door swung open to admit two men.

The first was Major Ruiz.

Behind him was a tall, fair-haired man the same height as Brand and could even have been his age. He wore an expensive light gray suit, a white shirt and a neatly knotted, thin dark tie. As he moved into the cell his gaze met Brand's and there was a moment in which the two men sized each other up.

'Sorry I've taken so long to get to you, Brand,' the man said in an unmistakable British accent. 'And I apologise for you having to be stuck here in this place. It serves a purpose but in your case it's less than suitable.'

'If that means you've come to get me out I'll agree.'

'That I have.'

'I don't know who the hell you are but you're a welcome sight.'

'Hunt. Captain Richard Hunt.'

Brand took the offered hand, feeling the latent strength in the man's grip. He judged Hunt to be a capable, reliable man. The kind who would be welcome in a tight corner.

Hunt turned to Ruiz.

'Major, your cooperation in this matter will be noted and passed both to your superiors and the British Consul.'

Major Ruiz inclined his head.

'Glad to be of help, Captain. If you learn more about this man, Han, please inform me.' He turned to Brand. '*Senor* Brand, my apologies for any inconvenience. I was unaware of your position in this matter.'

'You were doing your job, Major. No fault to be found there.'

Brand held out his hand and shook the Mexican's.

'Come on, Brand,' Hunt said briskly. 'I have a carriage waiting outside. We'll collect your belongings on the way.'

As he stepped out of the building Brand drew breath. The warm air held a tang of the sea. He paused for a moment to wait for Hunt. When he appeared he was carrying Brand's Colt and the Smith & Wesson. He passed them over.

'You might need these,' he said.

A carriage and pair waited for them. Brand and Hunt climbed in. As they settled in the soft seats the carriage moved off. Brand tried to relax, but found himself studying the man sitting across from him.

Hunt's clothing might have been fashionable but the man was no fop. He played the game well, hiding his toughness beneath a casual veneer. Brand was a good judge of character. He prided himself on knowing his man, whether friend or enemy. In his line of work making a mistake could easily lose him his life. If that happened nothing else mattered one way or another.

'If you don't mind, me saying so,' Hunt remarked, 'you look bloody awful.'

'Not been one of my better days,' Brand said. He was becoming increasingly curious about Richard Hunt. The vague thought flickered through his mind that perhaps Hunt was one of Han's employees; he dismissed the suspicion even as he conjured it up; Hunt was too perfectly in character, and head and shoulders above the sort who would sell himself to a man like Han. Despite that Brand still wanted to know who his companion was.

'I've heard a lot about you,' Hunt said. He leaned forward, a faint smile on his tanned face. 'How is Mister McCord?'

Brand became instantly alert. He hadn't been expecting such a conversation opener. For a second he was lost for words. Hunt had no such problem.

'The last time I was in Washington McCord and I had a chat about the Debenham affair. You were up in Montana working on that assignment at the time. A strange business. I'd met Lord Debenham a few times and when the complete facts came to light it was something of a shook.'

'You knew his daughter too?' Brand asked.

'Sarah?' Hunt nodded. He hesitated for a moment. 'A lovely girl. Terrible the way she died. I know she was helping you but I have no way of knowing how close you were.'

'Close enough that it mattered,' Brand replied. He didn't like dragging up the past. Especially when it concerned such a personal part of his own life. The feeling he'd had for Sarah Debenham hadn't died with her and it hurt when he allowed it to touch him.

For a time both men were silent. Brand stared out at the passing scenery. He saw little detail. The only thing be did register was that they seemed to be leaving Agua Verde behind, heading into the country.

'I have a *hacienda* a few miles out,' Hunt explained. 'The British Government rented it for my stay.'

'And how long's that going to be for?'

Hunt shrugged his broad shoulders. 'That depends on what you have to tell me concerning a certain Chinese gentleman by the name of Kwo Han.'

'Seems to me you already know a hell of lot I don't,' Brand said. He wondered just what Hunt was liable to come out with next.

'I have facts, but only from my side of the table. It seems that we can help each other.'

A short time later the carriage turned up a short drive and came to a halt outside the *hacienda*. The stone structure had been overlaid with plaster that had been painted a brilliant white, and the window, shutters, doors, and other woodwork had been done in a deep red. The house was surrounded by thick shrubbery and dotted with trees.

As the carriage stopped the front door of the house opened and a muscular black man stepped outside. He was dressed in a pair of canvas trousers and a cotton shirt, and he carried a huge old Dragoon Colt tucked under his belt. He stood watching as Brand and Hunt climbed down out of the carriage.

'He the feller, Cap'n?' he asked, his bright eyes studying Brand closely. His accent was odd to Brand's ears. A soft, rolling cadence Brand hadn't come across before.

'This is Mister Jason Brand,' Hunt said. 'He is, as we might say, in the same line of business we are.'

'Welcome aboard, Mister Brand.'

'This disreputable character is known by one and all as Rumboy,' Hunt said. 'It's a title he's acquired for his uncontrollable affliction to the wretched stuff be drinks. Stay round him long enough and you'll see what I mean. A habit he acquired back home in Jamaica. Apart from that he's a fair hand in a roughhouse and a pretty good shot with that blasted cannon he carts around with him.'

'I could have done with you a while back,' Brand said.

'From what I hear, boss, you done pretty good on your own. Those two boys you fixed up were bad fellers.'

'Look, we can talk later,' Hunt suggested. 'I think our guest would prefer to clean up, have a meal, and then get some sleep. Rumboy, get the help organised. Plenty of hot water for a bath. I'll find a razor and some clean clothes. Does the idea appeal, Mister Brand?'

It did appeal. Brand couldn't remember the last time he'd enjoyed taking a bath so much. The sheer luxury of washing away the sweat and grime from his body, followed by the removal of the itchy beard from his face, did wonders for his moral. He cleaned the bullet burn on his shoulder and side and treated them with cooling salve Rumboy had supplied at Brand's request. And then there was the almost sensual pleasure of getting dressed in clean, fresh clothing. Hunt had provided underclothing, a pair of dark trousers and a white cotton shirt, clean socks as well. As Brand finished off brushing his dark hair Rumboy appeared in the door of the bedroom. He had Brand's boots, cleaned and highly polished.

'Now you lookin' better, boss,' the Jamaican said. He placed Brand's boots beside the bed. 'You go 'head and get some sleep, Cap'n say. I come back and wake you in time for dinner tonight.'

'Thanks, Rumboy.'

The Jamaican left, closing the door behind him. Brand turned towards the bed. He stretched out on it, and couldn't help comparing its comfort with that of the crude cot in the Rurales' cell. He closed his eyes and slept. His last thought before he blanked out was about his assignment and the man he was looking for.

His name was Kwo Han, the son of a poor dock-worker, who had learned at an early age that a man had one chance in life to make good. Watching his father struggle through each day, breaking his back and his spirit to earn enough to keep food in the mouths of his family had taught the young Kwo Han another lesson. That physical toil made no man rich or powerful. Not in the streets of Shanghai. There was money to be made in other ways. By trickery. By deceit. And by plain and simple stealing. Kwo Han learned these facts with ease and quickly turned his talents to good use. By the time he was ten years old he was an accomplished pick-pocket. He had also tried his hand at burglary, and had already gathered himself an ample reserve of money and other valuables. In his sixteenth year, yearning for greater glory, Kwo Han was presented with a rare opportunity. He was approached by a courier of the Shanghai Tong, the elite of China's underworld organisations. The Tongs, secretive criminal societies, were feared and respected by both sides of the law. They had their own rules to govern the behaviour of their members, and any Tong recruit learned these rules before anything else. To go against the Tong meant suffering and death. For Kwo Han the terrors threatened by the Tongs meant nothing. He knew that once he was admitted nothing could stand in his way. His assumption proved to be correct. In his first five years with the Tong he advanced rapidly. Initially he was given work as a courier but an incident involving members of a rival Tong revealed the violent talents of the young Kwo Han. His reward was promotion to the ranks of the Tong assassins.

He was given instruction in the use of the traditional Tong weapons and rigorous training in the martial arts. Kwo Han became a deadly and efficient killer of men. Time after time be proved his worth and his loyalty to the Tong. In his mid-twenties he had progressed through the lower ranks of the society to become a respected and feared Tong Master, one who no longer took orders, but one who gave them, and accepted no excuses for failure. His need for power and his desire to extend the reach of the Tong beyond the shores of China turned his eyes towards the great American continent. Kwo Han realised the potential presenting itself. He saw the countless thousands pouring into the vast, rich lands and he knew that there was a future for his organisation in the New World. San Francisco and the Barbary Coast were ready-made breeding grounds for the criminally orientated, and the Tong of Kwo Han quickly established itself. Gambling, prostitution, the distribution and promotion of opium addiction. These were only a few of the Tong's dealings. It was also involved in the control of Chinese labor, the supply of goods to Chinese owned stores. Additionally there was the fleet of fast clipper ships and passenger-cargo ships plying the numerous trade routes; as well as the normal and legitimate cargo there were items carried which never showed on the loading manifests: drugs, illicit liquor, guns, a varied selection of goods shipped without the knowledge of the authorities to avoid heavy tax and duty payments; gold and silver bullion, stolen in one country and sold in another where the exchange rate was much higher; and there was the human cargo, for although slavery had been officially abolished by the greater nations, there were those who still practised the degrading business.

Black men and women were shipped like so much livestock to the ancient and isolated ports along the coast of North Africa - and not only black slaves, for the robed and feudal Arabs had taken a liking to the pleasures of the fairer skinned; young and beautiful white women brought a high price, as they had and still did in China.

For Kwo Han the years passed quickly and profitably. Yet even at the height of his power he was still always eager to involve himself in something new. Any scheme which might add to his prestige and his wealth. As with the arrangement he had made with the man named Harvey Ruger. Two million dollars' worth of pure gold to be brought out of America and shipped to Mexico in one of Han's ships.

Once in Mexico the gold became Han's responsibility. He would arrange for its sale to one of his contacts in Europe. A man who would pay in cash and at the rate of exchange agreed Han would receive almost four and three-quarter million American dollars. It was a satisfactory arrangement which Han would complete by using the money to set up a partnership between himself and the San Francisco based American syndicate Ruger had put him in touch with. The Americans had the ability to reach right across the continent, as far as New York. Allied with Kio Han's exceptional transportation and distribution network, the partnership would create a vast and dominant criminal organisation capable of stretching across America, and as far as China, North Africa and perhaps in the future even into Europe.

The first part of the plan had worked to schedule. The gold had been located and started on its journey to Mexico. An unforeseen problem had arisen in the form of an American lawman who had discovered the whereabouts of Ruger and Sung Shan. It became clear to Han that the Americans wanted their gold back. The spoils of war to the victor. Even after such a long time had elapsed since the Civil War, the US administration – as with any government - refused to forgive and forget. Born out of the desperation of the national conflict, the Confederate gold was wanted for the coffers of the Union. Because of Ruger's failure to deal with the man, and despite his eventual capture, concern had been raised over the possibility of the lawman having passed on information he might have picked up. Sung Shan had decided to keep the man alive, even to the extent of bringing him to Mexico so that he could be questioned thoroughly. But the American had managed to escape shortly before the ship dropped anchor, and had reached the shore safely, finding cover in the forest edging the beach.

Despite a search by Kwo Han's men the American had stayed free. He had inflicted fatalities upon Han's men, and had killed two more men shortly after he had arrived in Agua Verde before falling into the hands of the *Rurales*.

The whole affair had angered Kwo Han greatly. Not only had his organisation been compromised but he had been made to look a fool through the incompetence of his men. One man, a stranger to the area, had created total disorder. Kwo Han would have liked him dead very quickly but he had to proceed with caution. He could not afford to let the American damage his forthcoming business deal. He was concerned because the American had come into contact with a British agent called Hunt.

It was not the first time Kwo Han had been involved with the British. His criminal ventures had drawn him to the wide expanse know as the Caribbean and much of it was favored by the British. Their Empire still exerted great influence and they had a reputation of being ruthlessly single-minded when it came to protecting their own.

Kwo Han and Richard Hunt had crossed paths before. Each man was clever in his own way and despite their efforts neither had been able to overcome the other. Hunt, aware of the delicate nature of politics, had been forced to step back whenever he failed to gather enough evidence to lay at Han's door.

Han's endeavour in Mexico had not gone unnoticed. The British had their undercover agents spread over the Gulf area. So it had not been a great surprise when Hunt had shown up in Yucatan. He had close contact with the local law force – in this instance Major Ruiz of the *Rurales*. Hunt had to step carefully until he had solid evidence against Han, and the Chinese, aware of this, made sure he operated carefully. It had been the usual game of cat and mouse.

Han was mindful that Hunt would stay on his trail. His dogged single-mindedness would keep him in Han's shadow until he had destroyed him. Han had already realised that the events which had taken place could make life difficult for him. Any careless mistakes would be grasped at by Hunt. He would be watching and weighing the facts. Han would be forced to tread a delicate path. But he had no choice in the matter. He had to go through with his deals. Too much effort and expense had been expended, and the stakes were far too high to even consider pulling out. Kwo Han was not thinking along those lines. As far as he was concerned the situation simply called for further arrangements to be made, and to that end he had already made preliminary moves.

He glanced up from the papers he was working on when he heard the single, sharp tap on the door of his book lined study. Kwo Han pushed the papers aside. He rested his large, muscular hands on the polished surface of his huge desk.

'Come,' he said.

The door opened to reveal a heavy-set Mexican wearing a sombre black suit. The man stepped into the study, closing the door behind him, and crossed to stand before Kwo Han's desk.

'Sung Shan made it sound urgent,' he said.

Kwo Han nodded. 'Sit down, Cruz, and listen,' Han said. 'Yesterday an American shot and killed two of my men in Agua Verde. I presume you have heard about it?'

Cruz's eyes glittered. 'I heard. He is a *pistolero*.'

'I am not concerned with his ability to use a gun. Just the speed with which we can stop him using it again.'

Cruz's dark face hardened. 'You want him dead?'

'Yes. First, however, I would like to find out if he has passed on anything to that Englishman Hunt.'

Cruz grinned, showing his large, white teeth. 'You mean *The Captain*?'

'Yes. A most clever man, Cruz, who seems to have a great deal of influence with the authorities. Beneath his rather casual exterior there lies a very dangerous threat to my business in Agua Verde.'

'Is he some kind of policeman?'

'Something of the kind. An agent who works for the British. He spends a great deal of time in the Caribbean. And now Yucatan. It is not the first time I have come up against him,' Han said. 'Captain Hunt, for all his pretence, does a great deal of prying. He asks lots of questions, innocent on the surface, but by the time he has all his answers the result is far from innocent.'

'It could be why he took the American from the *Rurales*.'

'I do not think he did it because he has a soft heart. That man, Brand, has been plaguing me all the way from America. Another government agent.'

'What do you want done?' Cruz asked.

Kwo Han sat back in his chair. 'Hunt's curiosity is such that it would not take a deal of arousing. If he thought he might be able to acquire some important information concerning me, I'm sure he could be lured to a conveniently quiet spot.'

'And then brought out here?' Cruz grinned again. The idea appealed. 'We could use our informants make Hunt believe they are willing to pass him information.'

'Imaginative thinking, Cruz. Do it as soon as possible. I would like to have this matter settled before the buyers arrive. Remember, Cruz , I need the man alive. I do not mind how bruised he is as long as be will be able to answer questions.'

Cruz stood up. 'What about the American?'

'I think that we can leave him for a time. He will not be going anywhere. By now, he and Hunt will have exchanged any information they have, so his threat has been reduced to mere physical violence. At this point Captain Hunt takes on a greater potential threat. Therefore, Mister Cruz, we will deal with him first. Take him out of the game before he can instigate any action against me. The American will no doubt start looking for Hunt if he vanishes. If we work this correctly *he* will come to us. And then we will be able to deal with both of them at our leisure.'

'Then Hunt is yours,' Cruz said. He turned and left the room without another word.

Eleven

Kwo Han sat and stared out of the window. Out across the wide lawns beyond the sprawling hacienda the lush vegetation of Yucatan spread for miles into the hazy distance. At the back of his mind was the thought that he might have to leave Mexico long before he had intended. The possibility annoyed Kwo Han. He had taken a liking to the place. In his life he had travelled extensively, to many different countries. Of them all Mexico, left an impression on him. Especially this corner of Yucatan, with its pleasant climate and the availability to the Caribbean and America. One day he would have to find a permanent base for himself, and here would have suited him. But if things went wrong for him now that would be out of the question. He considered the money he'd invested here. The plantation, where he was now, with its flourishing fields. It would be a shame if he had to give it all up. Kwo Han slammed his fist down onto the desk top in anger. *No.* He would not give it up, at least not without a fight.

The door opened and Sung Shan came into the room. There was an inner satisfaction to be had, Kwo Han realised, when he looked on Sung Shan's suffering. Shan, faithful-to-death, as any Tong member had to be, took his recent failure extremely personally. Of all the Tong men in Han's employ, Sung Shan was by far the best, and in all his years he had never once made a mistake. Until now. Had it been any other man Han would have killed him on the spot. But Sung Shan was special, and Han knew he would never find another so capable. He had realised that to let Sung Shan live was the best thing he could do. Shan would be grateful and he would also be aware that his continued existence depended on his future performance. There would also be the determination to serve with even stronger devotion.

'Master Han,' Sung Shan said.

'I have been considering the events that led up to the American's arrival here. If that fool Ruger had made certain of the American's death I would not now have the complications that are bothering me.'

Sung Shan regarded Han in silence. He wasn't sure what was expected of him at this moment in time. He was also held back by a cautionary reluctance to say anything that might anger Kwo Han.

'It has occurred to me, Shan, that now the gold is in my possession and the two representatives of the

American syndicate are here, Mister Ruger's presence is superfluous.' Kwo Han stood up and walked slowly to where Shan waited. 'Let us face facts, Sung Shan. Ruger has proved, by the killing of his own former colleagues, that he is not a man to be trusted. He is also a man of extremely reckless actions as has been proved by his failure to kill the American, Brand. Such a man is dangerous. He could cause a great deal of harm at a time when too much has already gone wrong. I would not wish for such a thing to happen. Mister Ruger is ruled by his greed for wealth, and such men cannot be given too much freedom. It would be wise, I think, if he was rendered harmless.'

Sung Shan nodded briefly. He knew he had been given a command. The matter did not have to be spelled out for him. He had realised Kwo Han's train of thought from the moment the Master had started to speak. As he turned and left the study, closing the door quietly behind him, Sung Shan smiled to himself. Kwo Han had offered him a chance to make a small redemption. He would not fail the Tong Master this time.

Chu was waiting for him in the hallway outside the study. Sung Shan lifted his hand in a quick gesture and Chu fell in behind him. Sung Shan led the way across the hall and up the wide stairs to the next floor. He moved swiftly along a corridor until he was outside a certain door. Turning to Chu he spoke a few words. Chu reached inside his clothing and drew out a small, razor-sharp hatchet, the traditional weapon of a Tong killer. He passed it to Shan, who held the weapon out of sight as he turned and opened the door.

Harvey Ruger glanced up as Shan entered. He was slumped in a seat by the open window, sweat beading his face. A bottle of whisky stood on the small table next to his seat and Ruger had a glass in his hand. He stared at Shan through bleary eyes.

'Hell, it's the big man's errand boy.' Ruger's words rolled out in a slur of sound. He lifted his glass and drained it. 'Ain't you got anything else to do 'cept keep botherin' me?'

Sung Shan crossed the room and stood before Ruger's seat. He stared at the man silently until Ruger began to feel uncomfortable.

'Cut it out, Shan,' he grumbled. 'Ain't I got enough to put up with? Stuck here in this damn room because the big man downstairs don't want anyone wandering round. Hell, it's like bein' in a damn cell. An' when's he goin' to send them women he promised? Been so long since I had one I could start getting' ideas about you.'

'You have no need to worry any longer, Ruger,' Sung Shan said. He savored every word. 'Master Han has decided to solve the problem of your discontent. I am simply the bearer of the solution.'

Suspicion was already forming in Ruger's mind as he raised his head. There had been something in Sung Shan's words that unsettled him. He had no time to query the matter. As Ruger looked up Sung Shan's hand appeared, and the keen blade of the hatchet gleamed for a fleeting instant in the bright sunlight. Then the edge of the blade passed across Harvey Ruger's throat. It bit deep, severing everything in its path. Sung Shan stepped to one side as blood spurted from the ugly wound. He watched as Harvey Ruger died, his body sliding from the seat onto the floor, his blood spreading across the polished wood.

When it was all over Sung Shan left the room. He returned the hatchet to Chu, and gave him instructions concerning the removal of Ruger's body. Then he made his way downstairs again to report to Kwo Han that his wish had been carried out.

Twelve

When they had finished their meal Jason Brand and Richard Hunt took coffee and cigars on the roofed veranda at the rear of the *hacienda*. Beyond the soft light of the oil-lamps the night was black. The heavy scent of many flowers hung in the warm night air. For a time the two men simply sat back, enjoying the calm. Brand had learned to make the most of any offered moments of relaxation. In his life they were very few and there were long periods between each quiet moment.

'I have the distinct feeling that this time Mister Kwo Han isn't going to slip through my fingers,' Hunt said suddenly.

'Sounds like you've tried before.'

Hunt laughed softly. 'I wish I had gold ingot for every time I've failed. I'd be a rich man.'

'The way you've been talking about him makes him out to be a tricky bastard,' Brand said.

'Oh, he's smart, I don't deny it.' Hunt sat up, jabbing his cigar towards Brand. 'You ever had anything to do with the Chinese Tongs?'

Brand shook his head. 'I've heard talk. Never had contact though.'

'Then you can't realise the kind of people they are. Ruthless isn't a big enough word. But that's what they are. Completely ruthless. Fanatical to a degree. A Tong is a totally dedicated organisation which concerns itself with crime. With anything you think of from petty-crime right up to murder and extortion.

'Kwo Han's taken a liking to Mexico. He doesn't have much in the way of competition. There is also the fact that he's pretty well surrounded by potential customers. To the north he's got the complete American continent. After that there's a whole world waiting. I'm involved because he's even made sorties into the Caribbean. Jamaica especially and we British get touchy about our colonies.'

'You're telling me? Still we got our revenge at Boston.'

'I'd hoped that was forgotten.'

'Usually is except once a year.'

'Good. Now, Han is causing the USA and Britain problems all round.'

Brand smiled thinly. He lifted his coffee cup. 'So all we have to do is close the door on him. Just like that?'

'I didn't say it was going to be easy, old boy.'

'Hell, I thought you did.'

Hunt laughed softly. 'Never did believe that story about you Americans not having a sense of humor.'

'We also speak English,' Brand said.

'Well, almost.'

'So where do we go from here?' Brand asked. 'We have Ruger and the gold here in Mexico. This Kwo Han character is involved, and so are a couple of San Francisco hardcases. It must add up to something. A deal of some kind. But what?'

'On the information I have, plus yours and the material McCord sent me, I can only hazard a guess, Jason. Tell me what you think. We have Kwo Han and a group of organised criminals from San Francisco, who by the way, happen to have connections with people on the American East coast. I think there is a merger on the way. A partnership between the two parties. The gold to be used as finance for the deal. By the time Kwo Han's finished with it he will have it converted into American currency. Money that can be passed without problems. It's a sad fact, Jason, but a true one, that crime is becoming organised in the highly populated parts of the world, and especially in America. And people like Kwo Han, professional criminals, have already seen the way things are going. If they get on the roundabout now they are going to end up very rich and very powerful.'

'I hate to say it but you've made a hell of a lot of sense.'

Hunt frowned. 'I was afraid you'd say that.'

'Next question is can we touch Han?'

'Going by the book he's done nothing wrong until we can prove it. You know the law as well as I do, Jason, and if you think the American way is complicated you ought to read the British rule book.'

'That's where I don't have to worry,' Brand said. 'First thing I did when I joined up with McCord was to throw the rules out. Only one I work by is *make sure you hit him before he hits you.*'

'A man after my own heart,' Hunt grinned. 'If I had a glass I'd drink to that. To hell with fair play, let's get the buggers.'

'Let's not forget the gold,' Brand said. 'The US Treasury will never forgive me if I don't take it home.'

'No problem. Wherever the gold is we'll find Kwo Han.'

'Depending on how long he hangs on to it. Don't forget this deal he's got set up.'

'Kwo Han can't do anything until his buyer arrives. My information is that Han's customer won't get to Agua Verde for at least four days. I even have a name and a description of the beggar. He's a slippery Frenchman by the name of Christian Dupre. A very well known dealer in stolen gold, silver, precious stones. He's known to operate in Europe and more importantly London. London is a place where Han does a lot of business. As I was saying over dinner, Kwo Han is a man of varied talents.'

'You figure we should lay low until Dupre arrives? Then make our move?'

'Jason, we're in this together. Right down the middle. We both agree on our course of action.'

'Then, Richard, *old chum*, we wait.'

Hunt stood up. 'Let's go and see if we can find, something a little stronger than this blasted coffee.'

They moved back into the house. Hunt poured them a couple of stiff tumblers of mellow whisky.

'Does the title go with the job?' Brand asked.

'What? Oh, *Captain*, you mean?' Hunt shook his head. 'That's a leftover from my Army days.'

'Cavalry?'

'Does it still show? But yes. Lancers, actually. Spent most of my time in India. Northwest Frontier mainly. Hindu Kush and the like. Bloody awful country to fight in, and made no easier when you're up against those damn tribesmen. Fine fighters, don't get me wrong, but I don't suppose the idea was for it to be like a picnic. Even so I found myself in a few awkward corners. Lost some good friends too. You must know how it is.'

Brand knew how it was. He'd lost a few people he'd liked himself. They were gone and he was still alive. He sometimes wondered why that was. He was no different to any of them. Certainly no better. In some cases the ones who had died were fitter people to go on living than he was, but for some reason he'd been left behind to carry the memories. The bitter echoes of something gone and lost forever. He swallowed whisky from the glass, hardly even aware of its taste as it went down.

Hell, yes, he knew how it was. *Damn right he did.*

'Have you been in the Army, Jason?'

Brand brought himself back to reality. He digested Hunt's question and shook his head. 'Did some scouting for them in New Mexico against the Apache. Stuff like that.'

'Is it true what I've heard about the Apache? That there're few to touch them?'

'Not much left to touch any more,' Brand said. 'Apaches are just about finished. They ran a good race but there was too much against 'em. Damn fine people, though. If they'd been left alone...ah, what the hell...it ain't going to do anybody any good no matter what I say. The Apache was finished the first time he made a deal with the whites.'

'You sound bitter about it. But I think I understand. You've obviously fought against the Apache yet you still find you have respect for them as a people.'

'That's what they are, damnit. A fine people too. I fought against 'em. I killed 'em. And I lived with them as well. Hell, they were no different to you or me. All they wanted was food to eat, a place to live, and a chance to see their young ones grow. Trouble was they just didn't get that chance. Too many greedy folk who came and looked at the land and wanted it, and who said to hell with the Apaches. It was a wrong thing to do. It just started a damn war.'

The conversation stayed in the same vein throughout the evening. It was something new for Jason Brand. He was usually reluctant to talk over past history, finding little to be gained from dragging up the past. But Richard Hunt talked his language. He was a man who was involved in a similar existence and it created a bond between the two men. They were two experts in a business that dealt in hardship, violence and sudden death. Trite as it sounded even to Brand, the phrase did nevertheless sum up his job. He only had to look back over the events of his current assignment to justify it.

By midnight Brand had already gone beyond caring what business he was in. The rest he'd had earlier in the day hadn't been enough to make up what he'd lost. The drink he'd consumed, which was far in excess of his normal intake, didn't help. He felt himself slump back in the big leather armchair, his eyes heavy, his mind beginning to wander.

'You look like a man who's more than ready to turn in, old boy,' Hunt said. His voice came from a long way off, muffled and seeming to hang in the air.

'Rumboy, come and give me a hand with our American chum. I think he's had too much of our Mexican fresh air.'

Brand didn't remember going upstairs, or being put to bed. Sometime in the early hours of the morning he turned restlessly onto his side and opened his eyes. The room was dark and still. He lay for a moment, aware of the dull ache deep in his skull. He could taste the sour leftover from the drink in his mouth. Slightly disgusted with himself he jerked the blankets round his shoulders and went back to sleep.

The next time he opened his eyes it was morning, the sun streaming in through the open window of his room. Brand sat up slowly until he found his headache had gone. He was still left with the evil taste in his mouth. Pushing aside the blankets he saw that he was still dressed save for his boots. They were beside the bed so he dragged them on, stamping his feet into the tight leather. He crossed to the washstand and rinsed his face. After he'd dried himself he made his way downstairs. He caught the smell of fried bacon and realised he was hungry. Perhaps it was a reaction to all the drink he'd taken.

Hunt was already seated at the table when Brand entered the dining room. He glanced up and grinned at Brand. 'Feeling better this morning?'

'Had to get better,' Brand said. 'It couldn't have got any worse.'

'If it's any consolation I had a rotten night myself.' Hunt poured black coffee into a cup for Brand. 'Once in a while it does no harm to relax.'

'You two was so relaxed last night I thought you was goin' to fall apart.'

Brand smiled at Rumboy's appearance in the doorway. The Jamaican was beaming all over his face. He came into the room and placed a plate in front of Brand. There were a couple of fried eggs and some thick slices of fried bacon.

'That all right, Mister Brand?'

'Thanks, Rumboy.'

'Take your time, Jason,' Hunt said. 'If you want a horse to use later on Rumboy can fix you up.'

'You sound like you're going somewhere.'

Hunt nodded. 'Yes. I'm going to do a little snooping around today. See if I can pick up anything about Kwo Han and his gold.'

'Need any help?' Brand asked.

'No, but thanks, Jason. I know a number of people who, luckily for me, seem to pick up a fair amount of talk here and there. It's surprising what you can get from a single source.'

'I'll see you later then. Might take a ride into town myself later. There's someone I'd like to surprise.'

'Your Angel?'

'I told you about her did I?'

Hunt smiled. 'You did that, old chum.'

After breakfast Brand wandered through the house until he located Rumboy. The Jamaican was sitting at a small table with Brand's Colt and the Smith and Wesson stripped down. Rumboy glanced up at Brand's appearance and indicated the guns.

'Captain said you might be wanting to have these with you.'

Brand pointed to the Colt. 'Only that one,' he said. 'Other one I took off one of Han's boys. You can have it if you want.'

Rumboy shook his head. 'No thanks, boss, I'll keep the one I got.' He tapped the butt of the big Dragoon he carried. 'This old bird looked after me a long time and we know each other too well.'

It was the way Brand felt about the Colt. A gun he'd used often. That he carried with him most of the time. A weapon that had become so familiar to him using it was second nature. Closing his hand around the smooth-worn butt was like touching his own face. He knew its shape, its feel, its very being, and all without having to look.

'Captain put these out for you,' Rumboy said, pushing a box of .45 calibre bullets across the table. He watched while Brand completed the cleaning and oiling of the Colt, then reassembled the gun. 'Does it fire as good as it feels?'

Brand nodded. He thumbed brass-cased bullets into the Colt's chambers and gave it a final wipe with a rag. 'Hunt said something about a horse.'

'Sure, boss.' Rumboy got up. He dragged a squat, flat flask from his hip pocket, uncorked it and took a long swallow. 'You want to try some?'

'After last night? Hell, no.'

Hunt had left a dark jacket and a wide-brimmed white Panama hat for Brand to wear. Slipping on the jacket Brand felt something in the pocket. He pulled out a number of Mexican gold coins. It was obvious that Richard Hunt thought of everything. Tucking the Colt behind his belt Brand made his way through the house, emerging by a rear door into a paved area that led him to the stables. As he neared them Rumboy appeared, leading a frisky-looking gray horse.

'This feller be just right for you, boss,' the Jamaican said. He handed the reins to Brand and watched the American examine the horse.

'What the hell is that?' Brand asked finally.

Rumboy laughed. 'You foolin' me, boss? That's the saddle. One of the Captain's own.'

'The hell it is.'

Brand stared at the slender, almost minute piece of leather strapped to the horse. Did they really expect him to sit on the damn thing? There wasn't enough leather in it to make a pair of gloves. And no damned saddle horn at all.

Rumboy was grinning all over his broad face. 'Maybe you better walk, boss,' he said.

Brand grunted sorry. Like it or no, he was not going to let the damn thing beat him. If the British could ride around sitting on such things then so could he. He thrust his foot into the stirrup and pulled himself onto the gray's back. The horse sidestepped nervously as it felt an unfamiliar hand on the reins. Brand took up the slack and pulled it under control. He made himself as comfortable as he could on the saddle.

'You need me for any reason, Rumboy, I'll be at a Angel's *cantina*. You know it?'

'Sure do, boss.' Rumboy lifted his hand. 'Hey, you watch out for any of the Chinaman's boys.'

Brand took the gray away from the house and put it on the road that led towards Agua Verde. The day was bright, the sun hot on his face. He took time to look about him as he rode. There was no denying the natural beauty of Yucatan. All around him grew lush, thick greenery. There were any number of bright flowers as well. There were tall trees and graceful masses of soft tree ferns. Fruit seemed to grow in abundance and the dense forest just beyond the road held plenty of birdlife. Every now and then Brand caught sight of the sea, the blue water rolling in towards the shore. He saw the white surf, and suddenly he found he was reliving the terrifying time he'd spent in those waters himself. Tossed and thrown back and forth by the limitless strength of the inrushing water, his battered body no more than a chunk of driftwood to be played with until the sea tired of its game and cast him up onto the sand. From where he was now the water looked bright and blue and beckoning. It had looked and felt entirely different before. It was one of lifes tricks, he thought. There were two sides to everything. It all depended on which side of the fence you were standing at any one time.

He reached Agua Verde and located a stable where he could leave the gray. The place was run by a skinny Mexican who answered Brand's questions, then directed him along the street. Wandering in the general direction shown to him Brand found himself on the waterfront after a few minutes. He strolled along the cluttered harbour, studying the various ships tied to the quayside. There were a couple of tall-masted schooners, an old island trader with its paint practically gone and its sails a patchwork of faded canvas. There were numerous small boats riding the midday swell. There was no sign of *The Gulf Queen*. White gulls swept back and forth across the sky, filling the already noisy air with their raucous cries.

Facing the harbour was a mix of buildings. There were warehouses, shipping-offices, sail makers, and taverns. Brand walked by a number of them before he found the one he wanted. Angel's *cantina* was jammed in between the offices of a shipping company and a clothing store. Pushing open the door Brand stepped inside the *cantina* adjusting his eyes to the murky interior.

The place was half full. Most of the customers seemed to be sailors of various nationalities. Brand eased his way through the crush, managing to find an empty table in one corner of the room. He'd barely sat down when a girl appeared at his side.

'Is Angel around?' Brand asked in halting Spanish.

The girl, young and attractive, gave him an angry look. 'Something wrong with me?'

Brand shook his head. 'No. But I want to see Angel.'

'You and half of Agua Verde,' the girl muttered. 'What does she have that makes her so popular?'

'She doesn't ask too many questions for a start,' Brand snapped. 'Now go and tell her she's wanted.'

He sat and waited. After a few minutes Angel pushed her way through the crowd of customers and stood at his table. It was plain that she hadn't recognised him. The last time she'd seen him Brand had been dressed in rags, his face battered and covered by a matted beard.

'You want a drink?' she asked.

Brand shoved the Panama hat away from his face. 'That'll do for now,' he said.

A smile spread across Angel's face as she realized who he was. She leaned across the table and threw her arms round Brand's neck, kissing him fiercely.

'I heard there was some shooting,' she said eventually, slipping onto a chair next to him. 'Somebody said two men were killed. I tried to find out what happened but nobody would tell me any more.' She studied him gravely, a smile touching her mouth. 'You look so grand now. All dressed up...'

'And nowhere to go,' Brand finished.

Angel put her hand on his, her face serious. 'Are you all right? What about Kwo Han?'

'His time's coming.'

'Have you found help?'

Brand nodded. 'Yeah.' He smiled. 'And I was lucky you found me when you did. That was a time I needed help, and you gave it.'

'I will be finished here soon. Then we can go talk somewhere. If you want.'

'I want.'

For the next hour Brand sat nursing a bottle. He didn't drink too much. He'd learned his lesson after the session with Hunt the previous night. While he waited for Angel he let his mind wander. Soon, he knew, things were going to start happening. Kwo Han had already revealed himself as a man not backward in getting things done, and from what Hunt had told him about the man, Han appeared to be involved in something far too big to be allowed to slip from their grasp. The man had a large consignment of gold on his hands. Too valuable to lose and at the same time difficult to move about. But if his means of hiding it were as efficient as his method of getting it out of New Mexico and all the way to Yucatan then he probably had no worries. By now, though, Kwo Han must have found out Brand's connection with Hunt, and he would be undoubtedly making plans to safeguard himself. Brand would have given a lot to know what those plans were. Maybe Hunt had found something out. The Britisher plainly ran an organization with just as much efficiency as Kwo Han's. If there was something to be learned Hunt would dig it out. Even so Brand found he was feeling slightly guilty at just sitting back, taking it easy while Hunt was out trying to pick up information. It didn't sit right with him. Time off was one thing but not while another man might be putting his life on the line.

Angel noticed his brooding silence when she finally came to the table. She studied him for a minute, glancing at the barely touched bottle. 'Don't you like our Mexican liquor?'

Brand raised his glass and drained it. 'Only reason I came here.'

'The only one?' Angel asked softly.

Standing up Brand took her arm and led her out of the *cantina*. Angel showed him the way to go and as they walked she again noticed his silent brooding.

'Something is wrong? Tell me, *hombre*.'

He turned his head to look at her. 'Tell the truth,' he said stiffly, 'I feel a damn fraud. Wastin' time wandering round while the man I'm working with is out doing my job and maybe getting himself...'

'If he had needed your help would he not have asked for it?'

He nodded. 'I guess. But it still doesn't feel right.'

'Do not worry. You cannot fight the world on your own.' She slipped a warm hand into his. 'Spend a little time with Angel and then you can find your friend.'

She led him along a narrow backstreet just off the waterfront. In an old, crumbling stone wall was a heavy wooden door. Angel pushed it open and Brand followed her through into an overgrown courtyard. They crossed the open area to a flight of steps leading to the second floor of the weathered building. A black mongrel dog, stretched out in a patch of sunlight, lifted its scarred head and watched them go up the stairs. Angel took him along the roofed veranda. At the end she opened a door and took him into the single room she rented while she was in Agua Verde.

'Not much but it is mine,' she said, closing the door behind her. It wasn't much. Just a medium sized room with a small stove in one corner, a bed pushed against the wall. There were a few other items dotted about the room, a pair of stools and a shelf on the wall by the stove holding a couple of cups and plates.

'And a place in the country for weekends,' Brand said.

Angel laughed softly. 'The hut?' She crossed to the small window and threw it open. 'I was born there,' she said. 'When my mother and father died it became mine. Am I not wealthy, Jason Brand?'

He didn't answer. Angel watched him and she could see the restlessness in his face. He was concerned about his friend. She knew it, and she also knew there was nothing she could do to make things any easier for him. Angel sighed. It was such a pity to have to let him go. Just when it seemed they might be able to spend a few pleasant hours together. But from what he had come to know of him Angel realised that with Brand his job came first. She went to where he stood and slipped her arms round his neck.

'Maybe when you have finished what you have to do you will come and visit Angel.' She kissed him lightly on the lips.

'Maybe I will.'

Brand put his hands on her firm hips, pulling her body against him. He crushed his mouth over hers and felt her quick response. Angel's body moulded itself to Brand's, a soft sound coming from her throat. But the next second she drew herself back, shaking her head.

'*No*. You must go. I will take your thoughts away from your important work. Only promise that you will not forget Angel.'

'That's one thing I won't do.' Brand turned towards the door. As he stepped outside he said, 'I know where to find you.'

He made his way back to the street and from there to the stable. Paying what he owed Brand mounted up and rode out. He knew now that he'd been wrong letting Hunt go off on his own. He just hoped that nothing happened to the man.

A couple of miles out of Agua Verde he became aware of a rider approaching him. It only took a moment for him to realise it was Rumboy. The Jamaican reined his horse in alongside Brand's, and Brand saw the troubled look in Rumboy's eyes.

'What's wrong?'

Rumboy pulled his straw hat off. His dark face gleamed with sweat. 'Boss, we got trouble.'

'Hunt?'

Rumboy nodded. 'Yes, boss. Some of Kwo Han's bully boys were waiting for him.'

'How?'

'After you left this morning I come into town. Met the Captain and he told me he got the word somebody want to see him. Some feller with information about Kwo Han. Now the Captain didn't want to walk into a trap so we fixed it that I go with him, only I stay way behind, out of sight. This meeting was at a place on the other side of Agua Verde. Old warehouse that nobody use any more.

Captain goes in but he don't come out for long time. By the time I manage to get close the Captain was gone. Taken out by a door at the other end of the place. I found the tracks they left and I went after them. This time I see 'em. Four Mexican fellers. They were putting the Captain into a wagon. Captain was all tied up but he was giving 'em a hell of a fight. Once they get him in the wagon they left. No way I could get to him without they see me. So I come lookin' for you quick.'

'Any ideas where they were taking him?' Brand asked.

'Chinaman has a big house on the plantation he owns,' Rumboy said. 'I reckon that's where they took the Captain. We can find out easy, boss.'

'How?'

Rumboy said: 'There was one feller in the bunch who didn't go with the wagon. He stayed behind for a while and then rode back to town. We can ask him, boss.'

'You know where to find him?'

This time Rumboy's smile was mirthless. 'Find Cruz? Hell, boss, that's no trouble at all.'

Thirteen

'This is the one, boss,' Rumboy said.

Brand followed the Jamaican's pointing finger. Through the gloom of the cloudy afternoon he could see the dull gleam of lamplight shining through a dirty window. The window was on the first floor of a rambling, deserted old house that stood at one end of a filthy backstreet. The street was in the worst part of Agua Verde. A tumbledown, forgotten section of the town where rats outnumbered people. Even the air held the mouldy stench of decay.

'He live alone?' Brand asked.

Rumboy nodded in the gloom. 'He's a queer one, boss, Cruz. Likes to live by himself. Work by himself too most of the time. Bad feller. He likes to kill people I hear. Since Kwo Han came to Agua Verde, Cruz has worked for him.'

They took the horses into an alley and tethered them. Rumboy led the way into the old house, Brand close behind. He had taken out his Colt, checking it briefly before he'd followed Rumboy inside.

'Mind the stairs, boss,' Rumboy warned softly.

As they moved upwards Brand could feel the entire staircase moving gently beneath his feet. On the landing Rumboy touched Brand's arm, indicating which way to go. Moving along the dark passage Brand spotted the pale finger of light showing beneath an ill-fitting door.

'You ready, boss?' Rumboy asked.

Brand nodded. He eased back the Colt's hammer, his eyes on Rumboy's figure. The Jamaican took a couple of steps back, then launched himself at the door. His left shoulder smashed into the door and it crashed open with a brittle sound. Rumboy's momentum took him into the room where he let himself drop to the floor. Before the door had swung fully open Brand followed Rumboy into the room, his eyes searching for the occupant. He caught sight of a moving figure. A broad-shouldered Mexican, naked to the waist, lunged at him. Brand caught sight of a raised hand holding a long bladed knife. He ducked in beneath the blade, slamming his right elbow into the man's stomach. The man grunted, twisting to one side, still slashing down with the knife. The tip of the blade caught the sleeve of Brand's coat but didn't touch flesh, and Brand pivoted on his heel, not wanting to give the man time to recover his balance. Brand wasn't quick enough. With catlike agility the man turned, his arm driving the knife straight towards Brand's chest. Pulling his own body round Brand felt the knife slide across his chest, the edge of the blade slitting his shirt and nicking his flesh. He clamped his left arm down across the man's wrist, pinning the knife hand to his body, and in the same movement he smashed the barrel of his Colt across the side of the man's neck. The man groaned once. His knees gave and he stumbled to the floor. Brand snatched the knife from his limp fingers and stepped back.

'You all right, Rumboy?' he asked.

'Sure, boss.'

Brand closed the door of the room. He indicated the man on the floor. 'Is that Cruz? If it isn't he's going to be a little upset with us.'

'Don't worry, boss. That's Cruz.'

'Get him on his feet then, Rumboy, I've got a couple of questions to ask him.'

Rumboy bent over Cruz. He grabbed the man's arms and hauled him upright, spinning him against the wall. Cruz put out a hand to keep from falling over again.

'Hey, what is this?'

'You mean you've forgotten already?' Brand asked.

Cruz stared at him, his eyes wild with anger. 'Forgotten? What the hell am I supposed to have forgotten?'

Brand brought his left hand up in a smashing blow that pushed Cruz along the wall. Blood burst from split lips as Cruz stumbled, trying to stay on his feet. He stared at Brand with wide-open eyes, dazed by the unexpected blow, and the violence that had driven it.

'You beginning to remember?' Brand asked.

'I don't know what you're talking about,' Cruz said. He touched his fingers to his bloody lips. He stared at the bright colour on his fingers. 'Damn you. Diego Cruz doesn't let anybody do that to him.'

For a moment Brand smiled, a distant expression which faded quickly. And then he hit Cruz again. A hard blow to the Mexican's stomach that doubled Cruz over, and as the man's unprotected neck was exposed Brand clubbed downwards with the butt of his Colt. This time Cruz was slammed face down on the floor. Brand handed his Colt to Rumboy, then knelt beside the groaning man on the dirty floor. Brand reached out and picked up the knife Cruz had dropped. He rolled Cruz over on to his back and before the man could move Brand had placed the tip of the knife against Cruz's throat. He put just enough weight on the blade to penetrate the flesh. A bead of blood appeared at the point. Cruz's eyes bulged with unconcealed fear. A sheen of sweat glistened on his dark face.

'*Jesus.*' Cruz's word came out in a soft hiss. 'Are you *loco*?'

'Now you're getting the idea,' Brand said. 'Stay clever, friend, and tell me where Richard Hunt is. Don't tell me any kind of lie. You do and I'll kill you.'

Cruz's eyes rolled to one side. He stared up at Rumboy. 'He is crazy.'

In answer Rumboy crouched beside Cruz. He lifted his big Dragoon Colt and placed the muzzle against the side of Cruz's head, easing back the hammer.

'Then I'm crazy too, Cruz, 'cause if he don't cut your throat I'm going to blow out your brains.'

'*Bastards.*' Cruz spat. But he knew his bluff had been called. 'I hope that Chinaman cuts you in little pieces. He's got Hunt at his house on the plantation.'

Brand stood up. He took his Colt from Rumboy. 'You were right, Rumboy. You know how to get us there?'

Rumboy nodded. 'Sure, boss, that's no trouble.' He indicated Cruz. 'What we going to do with him?'

'We'll hogtie him good and tight. Then you get the word to Major Ruiz that we need this one locking up in a nice cell until it's safe,' Brand said.

Rumboy shortly produced a length of coiled rope. He dragged Cruz into a corner and expertly bound his hands and feet.

'You want me to bring a couple of the Major's men here?'

Brand nodded. 'I'll stay close. Keep my eye on things until you get back. Then we can leave.'

Rumboy had glanced out through the window at the darkening sky.

'Looks like we going to have a storm, boss,' he said.

'Let's hope it's a heavy one.'

'Why, boss?'

'Only way we're going to get Hunt is to go in after him, and Han's sure to have his property well guarded. Especially if he's got that gold around. Big storm would give us some cover.'

In reality Brand knew they were likely to need a damn sight more than just a shower of rain. What they did require was a lot of luck, a quick hand, and a quicker gun.

Fourteen

Agua Verde lay a couple of hours behind them. Once Cruz had been taken into custody Brand and Rumboy had ridden out. Leaving the town Rumboy had taken them north, through wild, heavily forested country. There was no trail to follow. The Jamaican didn't seem to need one. He knew the terrain well. He also knew the unpredictability of the Mexican climate. The breeze that had sprung up earlier increased in intensity, and shortly into their ride, Brand and the Jamaican found themselves in the thick of a strong gale. Soon after the first drops of rain struck. Within a couple of minutes the rain became a downpour. The high wind drove it down through the branches of the trees and the sound of it drumming on the thick foliage became almost deafening.

'Hey, boss, you all right?' Rumboy yelled over his shoulder.

Brand could barely see the Jamaican in the gloom. He eased his horse up alongside Rumboy's. 'Yeah,' he shouted. 'Half drowned but I'll survive.'

A little time later Rumboy reined in his horse. He beckoned Brand closer. 'We about there now, boss. Better leave the horses and I'll take you in close as I can.'

They hid the horses in thick bushes, then pushed their way through the rain-soaked foliage. Rumboy strode ahead as if he was walking in broad daylight. Brand found his progress less casual. More than once he found himself stumbling over some object hidden in the darkness at his feet. He muttered a low thanks when Rumboy finally indicated it was time to stop.

'There she is, boss,' Rumboy said.

Ahead of them stood the sprawling stone edifice belonging to Kwo Han. A two storey *hacienda* with most of its many windows gleaming with lamplight. Studying it closely Brand found he was able to make out figures moving behind some of the windows.

'You ever been inside?'

Rumboy shook his head. 'No, boss.'

'They could have Hunt anywhere in that place,' Brand grumbled. He sighed to himself. Better get on with it. Sitting on his heels in the rain wasn't helping anybody. Whichever way he tackled the job he couldn't see an easy way through it.

'Rumboy, I want you out here. No point both of us going in there. If something goes wrong I need a helping hand on the outside.'

'Whatever you say, boss.'

Brand pulled out his Colt and checked it. He made sure he had extra loads in his pocket. 'Give me thirty minutes from the time I leave you, Rumboy,' he said. 'If I haven't brought Hunt out by then you get your butt in the saddle and get the hell back to Agua Verde. Get in touch with Major Ruiz. Tell him what's happened, and get help out here fast. I've got a feeling Kwo Han might start to figure he'll be better off somewhere else.'

Rumboy pulled a thick pocket watch from his pant's pocket. 'I'll do that, boss. You don't think I should start for town now.'

Brand shook his head. 'Give me a chance to try and get Hunt clear. If I can pull him out without starting too much of a war I'd rather. Never was one for getting mixed up with too many people if there's shooting going on. Man's liable to get shot by the wrong feller.'

'I know what you mean, boss.'

Brand gave a quick nod. Without warning he rose and slipped out of sight. The move caught even Rumboy by surprise. After staring about for a time the Jamaican settled himself with his back to a tree. Jerking his flask of rum from a back pocket he uncorked it, took a quick mouthful and settled back to wait.

When he was no more than a hundred yards from the house Brand spotted a guard. A slim, dark shape moving along the front of the house. As the figure passed a lighted window Brand saw the rifle he was carrying. He watched the figure move away from him. He wondered how many more there might be. There was no way of telling. It all depended on how secure Kwo Han was feeling. The man might have just two or three patrolling the house. But if he'd been worrying about the gold he might have a dozen on the go.

Flattened on the sodden ground Brand waited for a while. He heard nothing, and he saw very little. The rain, still slashing across the ground, had set up a fine mist which cut Brand's vision considerably. Cursing the weather Brand moved again. The final fifty yards to the house had to be across open lawn. There was no cover. Brand ran towards the house, hoping that the guard he'd spotted wasn't around. This was not the time to get caught. He felt the wind grab at the wide brim of his hat. Brand snatched it off before it sailed out of sight. The action was to save the hat from being deposited in the centre of a flat, green lawn, right where keen eyes could spot it.

He reached the front of the house and flopped against the stone wall. Even though his clothing was soaked by the rain he could still feel sweat running down his body. Moving along the frontage, ducking under windows he passed, Brand reached the corner. He moved along this part of the house until he was at the rear. Now he could look for a way in. He wasn't particular whether it was a window or a door, just as long as it led him inside the house.

The first open window he found was barely large enough to let him get his head through. Brand moved on, groping his way along the dark rear of the house. His progress was slow, hampered by the need to keep a constant watch for any more guards. The noise of the wind and rain ruled out any chance of his hearing them. His only safety lay in seeing them before he was spotted. Dividing his attention almost caused him to miss a window with a two-inch gap at the bottom. Peering in through the misted glass Brand could make out the low-ceilinged, cluttered kitchen. Across the room he saw the long iron cooking-range, hot coals glowing against the partially darkened remainder. Brand waited a couple of minutes, searching the shadowed kitchen for any signs of movement. He saw nothing but wasn't satisfied. Even so he gripped the window and eased it open. The moment he had enough gap he swung his legs over the sill and climbed inside, closing the window again.

After the biting cold of the storm the kitchen's warmth was almost sensual as it seeped through his wet clothing, touching his chilled flesh. Brand stepped back against the wall, keeping in the deepest shadow, and let his eyes become accustomed to the subdued light. Gradually he was able to pick out more details. The shelves and racks lining the walls. Long table in the centre of the room holding various pieces of kitchen equipment. He stayed where he was until he'd covered every corner of the room. Finally he was satisfied. Brand moved across to the range. He held out his hands to the warmth of the fire, working his fingers, and planning his next move.

Somewhere in this house was Richard Hunt.

The problem was where.

Every room in the house presented itself as a possibility. Hunt might be in the cellar. He could just as easily be on the top floor. Brand took his Colt from behind his belt, and eased back the hammer. He knew he didn't have the time or the opportunity to go wandering from room to room looking for Hunt. His presence in the house could be discovered at any moment. That left him with a need for direct, fast action. He needed the answer to a question. The only way to get that answer was one Jason Brand knew very well. The kitchen door opened onto a narrow passage. Halfway along the passage Brand found a door. He tried it and found it locked. He carried on to the end of the passage and found that the passage split. One direction led to another door after a few yards, the other carried on into eventual darkness. Brand chose the door. This one was not locked. He moved the handle gently, holding the door as it was freed from the latch. Brand let it open a fraction. Soft lamplight filled the narrow gap. No sound reached him, and after a moment Brand pushed the door open slowly, letting his body slip through the gap. He was in a richly decorated room, the floor laid with highly-polished wood, the walls panelled and hung with a number of oil paintings. The centre of the room was taken up by a long table surrounded by a couple of dozen leather-backed chairs. Ornate silver candelabra stood on the table. It was, Brand realized, the dining room. He was halfway across the room when he spotted the dull embers of a fire in the deep hearth. An idea rapidly formed itself in his mind. Something which might help to give him the time he needed.

Brand returned to the kitchen and began a search of the shelves. After a couple of minutes he found what be was looking for. He put away his gun and picked up two of the squat, gallon cans of lamp oil. Back in the dining room Brand removed the tops from the cans and began to splash the oil around the room and over the furniture. With the remainder he laid a trail to the hearth. Picking up a heavy poker Brand raked the glowing embers out of the grate. Nothing happened at first so he pulled out more embers. The oil smoked and then ignited with a soft pop, blue flame rising quickly, spreading across the floor in fiery fingers.

The way out of the dining room at the far end was by a pair of double doors. Brand eased one open and looked out on to a wide, spacious hall. To his left a staircase led to the upper floor. Off to the right was the house's main door, flanked by high windows facing the rain-swept lawns he'd crossed. The hall appeared to be deserted and Brand slipped out of the dining room, leaving the door behind him open. Already he could hear the rising sound of the flames, and the scent of smoke was beginning to taint the air.

Brand started across the hall, tensing abruptly as a door opened on the far side. He turned quickly, stepping into the shadow of the staircase. He flattened himself against the embossed wood panel, the Colt once again in his hand, fingers gripping the butt tightly.

The shout when it came seemed loud enough to raise the dead. Panic edged the voice of the Chinese who had discovered the fire in the dining room. Brand could only see a dark shape outlined against the orange glare of the flames revealed by the open dining room door. It could have been no more than seconds, though it felt like minutes, before the cries of alarm drew others to the scene.

Sweat, cold and clammy, broke out on his face and he felt his body stiffen. This was the critical moment when he might be discovered.

Brand sank further back into the shadows as a door to his right was jerked open. Bright lamplight spilled out on to the hall floor. Two figures froze in the doorway, and Brand recognised the faces instantly. They were the two men who had been with Harvey Ruger at the gold cache back in New Mexico. Dwyer and Remo. Brand smiled coldly to himself. He couldn't have chosen better for his purpose. He held back for a moment in case anyone else showed.

Remo stepped out of the room, staring wildly about. He held a bottle in one hand and from the way he moved it appeared as if he'd been drinking heavily. His partner, Dwyer followed him at a decidedly steadier pace. He was about to speak when he became aware of someone moving towards him out of the shadows. Dwyer glanced in the direction of the approaching figure. And then something warned him of danger. A yell began to form in Dwyer's throat but it was cut off before it developed. Something hard smashed against the side of Dwyer's skull. He felt a numbing pain explode silently inside his head. It was so intense that he didn't feel the second blow. Darkness engulfed him and he was unconscious before he hit the floor.

As Dwyer dropped Brand reached out and grabbed Remo's arm. He spun the man round, slamming him bodily against the wall, and rammed the muzzle of his Colt against Remo's throat.

'You remember me?' Brand asked.

Remo stared at him. His face was pale, sickly. His eyes fixed themselves on Brand's face. After a few seconds Remo nodded.

'Keep remembering,' Brand told him. 'I've reason enough to blow the top of your damn head off right now. So give me the right answer when I ask a question.'

'Ease off with that damn gun, Brand,' Remo groaned. Sweat was oozing from his face.

'Where's the man Kwo Han had brought here today? Hunt.'

Remo gestured with a trembling hand. 'Upstairs,' he said.

'You know where?'

'Yeah, yeah. For Christ's sake, Brand, I didn't have anything to do with it. It was Han's idea.'

Brand put his weight on the Colt, pressing it deeper into Remo's throat. 'I don't care who's idea it was. All I want you to do is to take me where he is. Now, mister, before I get tired of holding this hammer back.'

Remo turned as Brand shoved him towards the foot of the staircase. He knew the chance he was taking. Though most of the household seemed to be engaged in fighting the fire Brand knew he might easily walk right into any one of them. He just hoped that he could get himself and Remo up the stairs before anyone's attention wandered from the flames. Luck seemed to be staying with him. As he shoved Remo towards the foot of the stairs a gush of flame and smoke rolled out from the dining room, filling the hall with its acrid fumes. For a second Remo hesitated but Brand poked the Colt's muzzle into Remo's ribs with a savage gesture, and kept the man on the move. They started up the stairs. Brand prodded Remo constantly. For himself he just wanted to keep moving. He knew that someone could spot him at any second. If that happened it was going to become distinctly uncomfortable.

'You won't get away with a fool stunt like this,' Remo said suddenly.

They had reached the top of the stairs unseen. Brand indicated for Remo to keep on moving. He didn't waste time arguing with the man. Even though Remo's words held a possible truth. Just how was he going to get away with it? Until Remo had expressed the opinion Brand hadn't given it a second's thought.

'I'll worry on that one,' Brand said, scowling at the man. 'You just show me where they've got Hunt.'

Remo led the way along a corridor. So far along he pointed to a door.

'Anybody in there with him?' Brand asked.

Remo shrugged. 'I don't know,' he said. Both his eyes and his voice betrayed his attempted deceit.

The door before them was jerked open. The impassive features of Sung Shan stared out at Remo. 'Remo? What is happening? All the noise...'

Brand saw Shan's eyes flicker beyond Remo's shoulder to where he stood. He didn't wait any longer. Driving forward, his left hand planted between Remo's shoulders, Brand lunged into the room. His push catapulted Remo against Sung Shan, both men staggering off balance. As Brand cleared the doorway he ducked off to one side, his Colt thrust forward, his eyes searching the room.

The first thing he saw was Chu. The huge Chinese, his scarred face gleaming with sweat, lumbered across the room, his powerful arms straining against his tunic. He was brandishing a long-bladed knife. Brand didn't hesitate. His Colt blasted a gout of flame and smoke. The bullet punched a ragged hole in Chu's massive chest. But the Chinese kept coming, seemingly oblivious to the blood streaming from the wound. Brand stepped aside, but his heel caught the edge of a raised floorboard. He fell back against the wall, sensing Chu's closeness. The Oriental's free hand reached out and Brand felt the thick fingers grip his shoulder, and then Chu was lifting him, swinging him round. The room spun sickeningly. Brand felt Chu's fingers release their cruel grip. He was hurled across the room, his body brought to a brutal halt as he smashed against the wall. Pain burned across his back. Brand slumped to the floor, desperately trying to regain control of his senses. He rolled, twisting his body, blinking his eyes to clear away the red mist threatening to blind him.

'For God's sake, Jason.'

The shouted warning registered.

Hunt's voice.

Brand lifted his head, and threw himself away from Chu's grasping fingers. Bracing one hand against the wall he got his feet under him and shoved up off the floor. And then something closed around his throat, iron-hard fingers burying themselves in his flesh. Brand choked. His left hand came up and gripped Chu's knife wrist, but even as he closed his fingers around it be knew he wasn't going to stop Chu. He looked into Chu's cold eyes and he was certain be could see an expression of pleasure there. The brutal face with its terrible scar began to blur.

'Use the bloody gun, man.'

Brand had forgotten the Colt. Now he brought it up, his right hand thrusting it forward until the muzzle was against Chu's massive torso, angling towards the heart. His thumb took the hammer back, his finger touching the trigger. The Colt exploded, the muzzle-blast scorching Chu's tunic. Brand triggered again. The bullets ripped into Chu's body. Chu took a faltering step back, his hand slipping from Brand's throat. He turned away from Brand, his eyes settling on Sung Shan as the Chinese pushed Remo to one side. A slim-bladed knife appeared in Shan's hand. He stepped round Chu's bloody figure, his arm already raised. This time Brand shot him before he could release the knife. The bullet took Shan under the left eye, shattering the back of his skull on exit. Sung Shan gave a brief, high scream in the second before his life ended, his body hanging in the air for a moment. As Shan fell, Remo turned, lunging for the door. He flung it wide, running out into the corridor. He started to yell a warning. Behind him Brand snapped off a single shot. The bullet caught Remo in the left hip, the heavy bullet shattering the bone. Remo lost control of his movement, crashing against the wall. He fell hard, his leg twisted under his body.

Brand kicked the door shut. He took note of the heavy bolts at the top and bottom. He slammed them into place, then leaned against the door while he reloaded the Colt.

'Hope you don't go without me, old chum.'

Brand raised his aching head. In the centre of the room, seated on a plain, hard, wooden chair was Richard Hunt. The man's arms had been twisted behind him and his wrists tied with a length of cord. For once the Britisher had lost his elegant poise. Somewhere along the line he'd lost his coat. His shirt was ripped and bloodstained. Hunt's face bore the marks of a recent beating. Dark bruises blotched his flesh. His lower lip had been split.

Stepping away from the door Brand picked up the knife Sung Shan had dropped. Chu had curled up beside Shan's body, his great bulk now still. Brand automatically put his hand to his throat, wincing as his fingers came in contact with the bruised, tender flesh.

'For a minute I thought the big chap had you,' Hunt remarked. He flexed his arms as Brand cut through the cord around his wrists. 'Thanks, Jason. I'm afraid those chaps just didn't play fair.' The British agent crossed over to where Sung Shan lay. Reaching under the dead man's tunic he yanked a heavy revolver from the top of his pants. 'Ah, that's better.'

Brand was at the room's single window. He was vainly trying to open it. The window refused to budge. Brand swore softly under his breath. He turned and snatched up the chair Hunt had been sitting on and smashed it through the glass. Cold rain drove in from the darkness beyond. Brand leaned out of the window, feeling the wind slap at his face, the rain cooling his temper a little. Narrowing his eyes he peered down and saw that there was a ten-foot drop to the sloping roof of a long, narrow wing of the house extending from the main part of the building.

'Not the way out I'd choose normally,' Hunt commented. He grinned at Brand. 'But we're not exactly in a position to call a carriage to the door.'

Without further delay the Britisher swung his long legs over the sill. As he did there was a sudden pounding on the locked door. Hunt threw a quick glance in Brand's direction.

'They sound annoyed. Just what did you do? Set fire to the damn place?'

It was Brand's turn to grin. 'Yeah.'

Hunt's laugh was whipped away by the wind. The Britisher lowered himself by his hands and then let himself drop. Brand saw him hit the sloping roof. The wet slates gave him no purchase and Hunt rolled to the edge of the roof and out of sight. Brand jammed his Colt into his belt and climbed out through the window. The wind buffeted him cruelly, trying to tear his fingers loose from the sill before he was ready, and when he did let himself go he found he had no control over the way he landed. The roof came up to meet him and he hit it hard, the breath knocked from his body. He made a vain attempt at slowing his slide down the roof. But then there was no roof beneath him. He hit the ground hard, managing to relax his body enough to absorb most of the impact. Even so he felt a sharp stab of pain across his left side.

Fifteen

'J*ason*.' Hunt's voice reached out from the darkness.

Brand struggled to his feet. 'Here.'

The pale oval of Hunt's face appeared. He had a fresh cut above his left eye but seemed otherwise unhurt.

'I suggest we beat a hasty retreat,' he said.

Brand nodded. 'Good thinking.'

For a moment Hunt hesitated. 'Did you bring Rumboy?'

'He's over on the far side of the house,' Brand said. 'I told him to give me a half hour then get back to Agua Verde and get help. I hope to hell he's got sense enough to go sooner.'

'If I know Rumboy, he'll have heard all the racket and be well on his way. He has a unique sense of timing.'

'Let's hope it hasn't run out,' Brand said. 'Best thing we can do is head away from the house. Won't be long before Kwo Han works out where we are.'

They broke into a run, cutting across a paved terrace which gave way to wide lawns. Beyond the lawns rose the dark mass of thick foliage and trees. Brand had no way of knowing what lay beyond the trees, or even where their way was taking them. It didn't seem to make much difference. The prime objective was to get away from Kwo Han and his men. There was no doubt in Brand's mind now that as far as he and Hunt were concerned it had become a simple matter of staying alive. Kwo Han's order to his men would be short and direct.

Kill them both.

The Tong Master's existence in Mexico was threatened as long as Brand and Hunt were alive and capable of striking back.

With only yards to go before they reached the cover of the dense foliage a rattle of gunshots broke through the steady sound of the wind and rain. Brand heard the sodden thump of a bullet kicking up a chunk from the smooth lawn close by. He didn't waste time returning the fire. In this darkness it was unlikely he'd hit anything, and he didn't have the ammunition to spare. Trying to ignore the uneasy feeling that had developed in the pit of his stomach he ran on, following Hunt into the dark mass of foliage.

They paused for a moment to catch their breath. Hunt touched Brand's shoulder.

'Look at that,' he said.

Brand turned and saw the rising orange glow over the house. A writhing mass of flame gouging a ruddy hole in the black sky. Showers of bright sparks exploded every so often, and over it all hovered a pall of smoke.

'One way and another, old chum, we've pushed our Mister Han into a position where he's got to do something drastic.'

'I just want to be there when he does it,' Brand said. 'And I'd prefer to be alive as well,' he added, reminding Hunt about their pursuers.

The thick undergrowth made progress slow. The near-complete darkness didn't make it any easier. Brand glanced skywards and spotted a pale moon fighting to shine through the dark, massed clouds. He cursed the foul weather, hating the unceasing lash of the rain as much as the heavy wind. The ground underfoot was waterlogged, the earth turned to a sticky, clinging mud that caught at his boots and seemed reluctant to let go. The only consolation to it all came from the knowledge that Kwo Han's men were having to endure the same conditions.

Gradually the undergrowth thinned out. Brand noticed there seemed to be more water on the ground than seemed natural. The fact came home with a vengeance. As he put his foot down he realised there was nothing beneath it. Unable to stop himself he plunged waist deep in cold, dirty water. He heard a heavy splash close by and knew that Hunt had done the same.

'Watch your step,' Hunt called. 'Seems as if we've wandered into a blasted stretch of swamp. There could be quicksand. If you do get caught in some don't struggle. Only helps to bury you quicker.'

'That's a comforting thought.'

Testing the slimy bed of the swamp at each step Brand and Hunt slowly waded through the scummy water. Tall weeds grew high above the surface, their roots buried deep in the black mud below. Many of the trees had their roots below water too and their trunks were covered in an oozing fungus. Pungent gas, trapped beneath the mud, was disturbed by their passing. It rose to the surface in great bubbles, bursting as it came into contact with the air. The resultant odour was strong enough to make their eyes water.

'Hold it,' Brand called.

Hunt froze and they both listened to the not too distant voices calling back and forth in agitated Spanish. Brand eased his body round as he heard the rustle of weeds being disturbed. At that moment the moon broke through the cloud. Pale light silvered the gloom. A dark figure rose out of the weeds, the moonlight glinting on the barrel of a revolver. Brand saw the revolver swinging its muzzle towards him. He whipped his Colt round and fired. His shot threw a lance of flame into the darkness, the sound of the shot echoing out across the water. Somewhere a disturbed bird rose into the air, wings flapping in alarm, its shrill cry seeming to mimic the scream of the man hit by Brand's bullet.

'The bastards are closer than I thought,' Brand snapped. He plunged ahead of Hunt, his eyes straining to see through the shadows ahead, suspecting every movement, no matter how slight. He was on edge now, keyed up, and trusting no one except himself.

Yards to his right he heard the splash of someone jumping into the water. He caught sight of the widening rings of displaced water. Behind him he heard the click of Hunt's gun going on to full cock. Then the blast of a shot filled his ears. Hunt fired again and a man grunted. There was a frenzied splashing and then silence.

In the distance they heard more shouting. Some in Chinese, more in Spanish. Brand's limited vocabulary allowed him to pick up some of the Spanish. Simply translated Kwo Han's men were still searching for Brand and Hunt. The storm was making it hard for them and there was a degree of resentment at being out in the wind and rain and stuck in the swamp.

Brand felt no pity for the men. They were on a death hunt, searching for the two men who had escaped Han's clutches. Given the chance the pursuers would shoot down Brand and Hunt without a thought. So any discomfort they experienced was well deserved as far as Jason Brand was concerned.

Brand felt the water becoming shallower. The soft mud beneath his feet started to turn solid and after a few more minutes he gratefully waded onto firm ground, Hunt close behind. They didn't stop, but simply moved on, through the dense foliage and trees.

Another shot filled the night with its ugly sound. The bullet embedded itself in a tree only a foot from Brand's head. He dropped to his knees, crawling to the cover of a rotted log. Hunt stretched out beside him. The air was suddenly full of bullets. A ragged volley of shots ripping through the foliage and tearing white gashes in the tree bark.

'What do you think of Yucatan now?' Hunt asked dryly.

Brand didn't look up from reloading his Colt. 'It's just like home.' he said.

'At least we know where Han is.'

Brand grunted. 'Fat lot of good it's going to do if we don't light out of here.'

Twisting over on to his back Hunt studied the sky. 'Another couple of hours it's going to be dawn. We'll be able to see where we are.'

'And so will they. Either way we play it we end up with a lousy hand.'

'Do I detect signs of defeat?'

'I didn't think you British ever used that word.'

'You think?'

Gunfire filled the night with noise. Bullets chewed into the log, showering Brand and Hunt with rotted wood. As the blast of sound faded away Brand raised his head, straining his ears. He caught the soft sound of someone running, and knew he'd guessed right. The shooting had been a cover. Giving one of

Han's men the opportunity of reaching their hiding place. Brand listened for another second, placing the running figure. He leaned across the top of the log, levelling his Colt. A moment later the man was illuminated by a patch of moonlight. Brand recognised the face. It was Lex Dwyer. The heavy Colt in Brand's hand exploded twice. The bullets smashed Dwyer backwards. He twisted as he fell, hitting the ground on his face, the gun in his hand going off with a muffled sound.

'You want to stay here or chance moving?' Brand asked.

'I always feel better during a running fight,' the Britisher replied. 'Never have been able to just sit and wait.'

Brand touched Hunt's arm and pointed out the direction he intended taking. Hunt nodded. Together they rose to their feet, clearing the log, driving forward into the gloom. Ahead of them lay a dark spread of dense forest, an overlapping mass of trees and foliage. They plunged into the greenery, bullets snapping at their heels. Brand felt something tug at his left sleeve but it was the only bullet to come close.

They kept up the hectic pace for ten minutes. Eventually they slowed, allowing their tired bodies to rest. As they paused Brand realised that the rain had slackened, the high wind dropping too. It didn't stop completely but it was obvious that the storm's full power had been spent. There was still the steady fall of the rain against the dripping foliage and the ground underfoot was still sodden.

'It always happens like this,' Hunt remarked. 'A storm hits and while it lasts it really lets rip. Then it slacks off, ends, and a couple of hours later you wonder if it ever happened at all.'

Far behind them Brand could hear the sounds of their pursuers. Hunt had picked up the sound too. The cessation of the full storm was making it easier for their pursuers too.

'If we cut off to the east we should pick up a river,' Hunt said. 'Somewhere along it is a spot where it joins a road which will take us back to Agua Verde.'

Brand looked doubtful. 'I'd like to get hold of a horse as soon as possible.'

'*Oh?*'

'I'm trying to figure how Han's feeling right now. He'll be deciding what chances he has left. We know too much about his plans, and he'll be aware of that. He's got a damn great pile of gold he wants to sell, and a big deal ready to be made. He's going to figure the Mexican authorities may be about to close in on him. So I'm betting he's going to move that gold. Right now. If he gets it out of the country he'll feel safer. Somewhere along this coast he'll have that ship of his ready and waiting. He'll be forced to use it now we've forced his hand.'

Hunt stared at him for a moment, his face hardening.

'You're right, Jason. It makes good sense. He isn't going to sit and wait for everything to blow up in his face. It doesn't matter to Kwo Han where he makes his deal for the gold. It wouldn't even be too much trouble for him to sail right to his customer's back door. Bringing the gold to Yucatan was the easy way to remove it from US hands. He'll be figuring to move it away again.'

'Yeah? Well not if I've got anything to do with it,' Brand said with feeling.

Sixteen

Barely an hour had passed since sunup yet the oppressive heat was already making Brand sweat. He wished it was still raining. Since the downpour had stopped the heat had returned, drying their clothing and sucking the moisture from their bodies. He trailed behind Richard Hunt's erect figure, envious of the Britisher's almost casual disregard of the overpowering climate, but determined not to let his own discomfort show. To himself he admitted an obsessive longing to lie down and say to hell with it all. Not that he ever would. Brand was no different to anyone else. He had his weaknesses, his fears, but he kept them to himself and made a show of outer toughness. He often wondered why. *Vanity? A need to prove himself against an uncompromising world?* Or simply the camouflage required to enable a man to survive? The answer, whatever it was, never revealed itself too clearly. Hunt glanced over his shoulder, a smile showing through the grime of his face.

'There she is, Jason,' he said.

Following the Britisher's raised hand Brand caught sight of water glinting in the bright sunlight. Hunt had been right about the river. He'd been right about the distance too.

'How far before we reach that road?'

Brand still had the nagging feeling the longer they wasted out here, the more certain he felt Kwo Han was going to get away. He believed now that somewhere not too far away the Chinese was preparing to move his gold.

'Two, maybe three hours,' Hunt answered.

'Any chance we might be able to pick up a boat? Something to get us downstream quicker.'

Hunt didn't answer straightaway. Pushing through the foliage along the bank of the river he stood at the water's edge, looking first up and then downstream. He turned as Brand joined him.

'I wanted to make sure just where we are,' he said. 'If I'm not mistaken there's a small village about half a mile upstream. I daresay we could borrow a boat there.'

They moved off again, conscious all the time that somewhere behind them were Kwo Han's men. Since the gunfight in the swamp they hadn't had any more contact with the men chasing them. But they had heard them during the hours of darkness. Still following, though at a discreet distance now. When daylight had come Kwo Han's men had fallen even further back, not wanting to reveal themselves to the accurate fire of the two they were following. Their pursuers' caution had given Brand and Hunt a strong lead. They didn't however fall into the trap of becoming complacent. Both of them knew that Han's men were still on their trail, and they knew the penalties for over-confidence.

During the odd times they had rested during the night Brand had learned the facts concerning Hunt's capture by Kwo Han. The Britisher had done nothing to conceal the fact he'd made a bad mistake in letting himself walk in to the trap set by the Tong Master. Kwo Han had made it clear to him that Hunt's life meant nothing. He only required Hunt for the information be could impart. The Chinese, though he hadn't said it in so many words, had been obviously worried over his position in Yucatan. He needed to know how much Hunt was aware of, and to whom he had given his information. Hunt had maintained a steadfast silence. It had cost him a deal of discomfort, but staying silent and listening had furnished Hunt with enough facts to be able to realise his guess had been right. Kwo Han was contemplating a merger with an American criminal group. The gold was to be used as finance. Hunt had learned also, from a boasting Dwyer, that Harvey Ruger had been killed, leaving the way open to a fifty-fifty partnership.

The more Brand thought about it the more certain he became of the way Kwo Han's mind would be working. The Chinese, an old hand at survival, lived by his wits, his ability to keep one step ahead of trouble. He would have made his decision by now, based on the facts that both Brand and Hunt were free, capable of using the knowledge they had to harm him. Mexico's previous availability as a refuge had come to an end, and Kwo Han's very nature would prompt him to undertake swift action.

Hunt's low voice, taut with concern, broke through Brand's deliberations. He caught the Britisher's gesture for silence, and looked beyond Hunt's shoulder. Coming through the tangled mass of foliage and trees ahead of them was a band of mounted men. Brand swore softly, snatching the Colt from his belt.

Damn, did it never end?

How many more had Kwo Han sent after them?

But then he heard Hunt laugh. He glanced at the Britisher and saw the man's grin. For a fleeting moment be wondered if the man had gone crazy.

'It's Rumboy,' Hunt said. 'Damned if he hasn't brought half the *Rurales* force with him, too.'

Brand watched the riders approach, feeling tension drain out of his body. He let the Colt sag towards the ground. Hunt had been right. The riders were *Rurales*, and Major Ruiz was at their head.

'Hey, Captain. Mister Brand.' Rumboy's dark face split in a wide smile. He slid from his horse, coming to meet them. 'I sure hope you don't do things like this very often. All the time I been thinking we goin' find you dead.'

'We're all right,' Hunt told him. 'Listen, Rumboy, we haven't got time to waste. What word have you got on Kwo Han?'

'He's running, boss. Mister Brand's fire done burned him out.'

'You know where he's gone?' Brand asked.

Rumboy nodded. 'He left pretty good tracks. That wagon he took with him is leaving marks a blind man could follow.'

'You were right, Jason. He's taking the gold with him,' Hunt said. 'And he won't be able to move too fast. The ground will still be pretty soft after all that rain.'

'Where do you think he's making for?' Brand asked.

'I reckon Bay of Caves,' Rumboy told him. 'Nearest place for a big ship to come in close.'

'Same place I came ashore,' Brand said. 'Angel told me Bay of Caves.'

Hunt nodded. 'It's a likely place. Deep water and sheltered. Han's ship could get in and out without trouble.'

'He's got plenty of riders with him,' Rumboy said.

'It appears our Chinese friend has hired himself some help,' Hunt said. 'He had a bunch of Mexican guns with him at the big house.'

'You are sure?' Ruiz asked.

'Thats right, Major,' Brand said. 'There were Mexicans in the party chasing us through the night.'

'They are nothing but scavengers,' Ruiz said. 'Look at Cruz and you see them all. They swagger around believing they are old time *banditos*. They are nothing. Toss them a few pesos and they would slit the throats of their own mothers. If they had mothers.'

'Major Ruiz, I get the feeling you would be happy to get rid of them.'

'Agua Verde does not need these dogs. My predecessors did little to solve the problem, but I cannot stand around and let them plague us. They are like flies around a jar of honey.' Ruiz suddenly smiled. 'This could be the opportunity I have been waiting for. To catch them in a criminal act. It would give me the freedom to engage them and rid our town of their presence.'

'You're welcome to ride with us,' Brand said. 'We'd be grateful for your assistance.'

'Better a dozen than just three,' Hunt pointed out.

Ruiz nodded. 'You have convinced me.' He called over his shoulder. 'Sergeant, bring up those extra horses. Then have the men ready to ride at my command.'

A pair of saddled horses were led to where Brand and Hunt waited. They hauled themselves into the saddles. Brand felt more comfortable sitting the wide Mexican rig.

Major Ruiz told them that he and his men still had work to do at Han's former home, rounding up the people who had been working for him. It appeared that Cruz had been doing a lot of talking, implicating Han in illegal activities in and around Agua Verde.

'Nothing like someone wanting to save his own skin,' Brand said.

Rumboy grinned.

'I think it might be to do with him having been half scared out of his wits by Mister Brand.'

The *Rurales* Major directed a section of his troop to ride for the house and carry out the task, then turned back to Brand.

'Now we are ready.'

'Rumboy, let's ride,' Brand called.

Rumboy nodded and wheeled his own horse around and led the group across country. They pushed their horses hard, forcing a gruelling pace. It went against Brand's grain to misuse a horse, but he was driven by an almost desperate need to reach Kwo Han before the man had time to escape. The realisation crossed his mind that he had yet to come face-to-face with the Chinese. Kwo Han was just a name to him for the present. A mysterious figure lurking in the shadows handing out his instructions. Brand found he was becoming curious. He wanted to see what this man looked like. He found that he was cold as far as emotions went concerning Kwo Han. The man had proved himself to be totally ruthless...an unfeeling, calculating man who could order another's death without concern. He had done his best to have Brand killed. Now, maybe, the boot was on the other foot.

The landscape had taken on a fresh look following the storm, the green foliage interspersed with bright flowers and the whole radiating a lush aura.

An hour before noon they sighted the coast. Soon after Rumboy pointed out the wagon tracks in the still soft earth. They could also see the hoof prints from a number of horses that accompanied the loaded wagon. The riders rode in a tight formation, protecting the wagon.

'Bay of Caves just along here,' Rumboy said. He took them in amongst the trees bordering the shoreline and they dismounted. Ruiz ordered his men to do the same. Rumboy led them to where the greenery gave way to the steep slope leading down to the white beaches surrounding the wide, circular bay. They were able to see the whole of the Bay of Caves. It was a good half-mile across. A sheltered lagoon circled by a rim of white sand and a wall of weathered rock dotted by countless caves. Beyond the rock the greenery took over, trees and foliage spreading back on to, the mainland. Close in to the shore *The Gulf Queen* rode at anchor.

And two long rowing boats were pulled up to the beach. Both were heavily laden with wooden cases taken from a wagon standing near the water. A group of armed Mexicans clustered around the wagon.

'There they are, boss,' Rumboy said. 'All we got to do is stop them.'

Brand eased himself into a comfortable position against a tree trunk. 'Which one is Kwo Han?' he asked.

Hunt leaned forward, studying the figures crowded around the wagon and boats. 'The one in the brown suit. That's your big bad Chinaman.'

'This time he doesn't walk away,' Brand said. 'He's caused enough death and misery to get his hands on that gold. It'll be my pleasure to take it away from him.'

'I will take my men and we will come around from the other side,' Major Ruiz said.

'Go ahead,' Brand said. 'We'll give you a few minutes to get into position.' As Ruiz turned to go Brand called, 'Good luck.'

Ruiz nodded. 'And you.'

Brand watched as the *Rurales* led their horses back into the trees, waiting until they were some distance away before mounting up. The *Rurales* eased into the heavy thickets and timber, disappearing from sight.

'I hate this,' Hunt remarked, then added, 'Waiting, I mean.'

'We won't be doing it for long,' Brand said, spinning the Colt's cylinder to check it.

They allowed a few more minutes until Rumboy nudged Brand's arm.

There had been a sudden flurry of movement near the boats. Brand realised that they were being pushed away from the beach. He stood up, shrugging out of the jacket he was wearing, making certain he took the extra .45 bullets and dropped them in his pants pocket.

'You feel up to some exercise?' he asked Hunt.

The Britisher's bruised, unshaven face grinned at him. 'I do believe, Mister Brand, that you intend to cause discord and altercation amongst our brothers.'

'If I knew what you meant I'd probably agree.'

Rumboy shook his bead. 'I ain't sure I know what either of you is talkin' about, but whatever we goin' to do, how we goin' to do it?'

Brand didn't answer. He simply moved off along the tree line, keeping in the shadows where the sandy beach gave way to the greenery of the foliage. Hunt followed him and Rumboy brought up the rear.

They had only gone about thirty feet when, without warning, a Mexican carrying a rifle stepped out of the shade of a thick palm tree. He was no more than a few feet ahead of Brand, and there was no hope of avoiding being seen. Brand carried on moving forward, and as the Mexican started to glance in his direction Brand lifted his right arm, then brought it down in a brutal chopping movement. The barrel of the Colt caught the man just behind the left ear, dropping him instantly. But as he fell the Mexican jerked the trigger of his rifle and it went off with a blast of sound.

'*Damn*,' Brand said bitterly.

The figures by the wagon all turned towards the source of the shot. One of the Mexicans opened up with a rifle. Bullets peppered the sand around Brand. He pressed in close to the rough trunk of the palm, snatching up the rifle dropped by the unconscious Mexican. He put it to his shoulder, aimed, and fired. His first bullet ripped a long sliver of wood from the top board of the wagon side. The figures near the wagon scattered, a ragged volley of shots coming from their guns.

'Spread out,' Brand yelled. He lunged forward, seeking the cover of a boulder half buried in the beach, bullets chewing up angry gouts of sand close to his body. He hit the hot sand, hugging the curve of the boulder, wincing as he heard the high, vicious whine of bullets striking the rock. Dragging himself to one end of the boulder Brand poked the rifle into view. He spotted a slim figure racing along the beach towards his hiding place – this time one of Han's Chinese. Brand fired twice, putting the bullets close together in the chest of the yelling Chinese. The man was knocked off his feet, his body arching in pain as he struck the ground.

There was no time to see how Hunt or Rumboy were faring. There was no time for anything but trying to stay alive. Firing and firing again, Brand kept glancing out to where the two rowing boats were moving slowly towards the waiting ship. He thought of the gold on those boats, and all the misery and suffering it had caused. Too many people had died because of it to allow it to vanish again. He turned his attention back to the wagon. Two more of Kwo Han's Mexicans were down. Even as he looked another fell back, blood squirting from a wound in his throat.

From the wagon came a heavy burst of fire. Brand drew back into the shelter of his boulder, bullets striking the hard rock. Stinging chips of stone peppered his face. He rolled to the other end of the boulder, peering round the edge. Three Chinese were coming along the beach. They were moving fast, in a zigzag pattern that presented a difficult target. Brand saw movement off to his right. He saw Richard Hunt, up on one knee, his revolver gripped in both bands, taking steady aim. The Britisher ignored the bullets coming his way. He held his ground for long seconds before he fired. His single shot took one of the running Chinese in the head, the impact of the heavy bullet seeming to tear the man's skull wide open.

While the Chinese was still falling Brand dropped a second man with a bullet through the leg. The Chinese fell heavily, his body twisting in pain, but still tried to use his rifle. Brand shot him again and the man became still. The remaining Chinese reached Brand's boulder before he was stopped, bullets from both Hunt and Rumboy ripping into his body.

And then Ruiz and his band of *Rurales* came galloping into view, pushing their horses hard and firing as they came. The Mexican bandits turned to engage them and the beach area erupted with the harsh crackle of gunfire. Men and horses were screaming as bullets found their mark. There was no distinction in the thick of battle. Bullets carried no conscience when it came to inflicting damage.

The violent exchange of fire, the swirl of powder smoke, the reek of death was a frantic panorama for everyone involved. It was not a place for the fainthearted. The lack of compromise was absolute.

Each man, from whichever side he came, struggled to the same end. His own survival and the death of the enemy. In that frame of mind there was no room for good intentions, or staying the hand, or voicing concern over the other. Blood for blood, bullet for bullet, the opposing sides waged their isolated little engagement until the final bullets were fired and the churned sand was dappled with spilled blood and the wretched bodies of the dead. Although the main victory went to Ruiz and his *Rurales*, his force was not without loss. Two men were down and would not be standing again. Three more were wounded. Kwo Han's own Chinese and his mercenary Mexicans were all dead, scattered around the wagon they had been defending.

As the firing came to an end it became very quiet. Brand tossed aside the empty rifle and took out his Colt. He stood up slowly, his eyes on the empty wagon. He could see only one figure behind it now. A broad, erect shape. Bareheaded and wearing a brown suit.

Kwo Han.

Brand approached the wagon. He sensed Hunt and Rumboy just beyond him. The sun was warm against his body and he could feel the heat from the sand burning through the soles of his boots.

Kwo Han's figure stepped out from behind the wagon. Brand tensed, his finger easing back against the Colt's trigger. But Kwo Han was not even looking at him. The Chinese had turned to face the water. His words when he spoke rang clearly out across the placid surface of the bay. Brand couldn't understand the language but he was made quickly aware of the meaning.

The two Chinese in each of the rowing boats rose to their feet, abandoning their oars. They began to rock the heavily laden boats from side to side. Water spilled over the sides.

'*What the hell*,' Brand yelled.

'They're sinking them, boss,' Rumboy said. 'Capsizin' the boats.'

The first boat tipped to one side as the heavy cases of gold shifted. The two Chinese dived clear and began to swim out towards *The Gulf Queen*. Already the clipper had begun to raise its anchor. The calm water of the bay foamed as the dead weight of the cases slid from the overturned boat. They sank immediately. The second rowing boat sank stern first as water surged in, the weight of the cases dragging it beneath the surface.

Rumboy sighed. 'Hell, boss, it's gone.'

'What do you mean?' Brand demanded.

'Ain't nobody goin' to get that gold now, boss. Too damn deep here. I talked to people about this place. This bay, she go down twenty, maybe thirty fathoms most places I heard. Bottom, *ahh*, she full of big holes. Ain't nobody been able to find out how far down.'

Jason Brand stared at the blue water of the bay. Already the disturbance had vanished, the foaming water settling, leaving the surface as placid as it had been before. He felt a momentary anger at the loss of the gold, but it faded just as quickly. There was nothing he could do about it. If McCord wanted his gold he was going to have to come and get it himself. It was ironic. The gold had been lost at the start of his assignment and now it was lost again. For all the good it had achieved it might as well have stayed where it had been back in New Mexico. If it had a number of people might still be alive. The Confederate gold had cost a great deal in human suffering and spilt blood.

Had it been worth it, he wondered?

'Well, old chum, at least we put a stop to Han's empire of crime,' Hunt said. 'Once we get him behind bars the rest of his organisation will fall apart. That should keep both our governments happy.'

Brand drew his attention back to the waiting figure of Kwo Han. The Chinese returned his stare with stony indifference. It seemed strange to be finally face to face with the man who had engineered this whole episode. Brand could see why Kwo Han's employees had been so fiercely loyal. The Chinese made an impressive figure, silent and still as he was. It was easy to see why he'd been able to instil such fear in those who worked for him.

'I congratulate you, Brand,' Kwo Han said in perfect English. 'Now I can see why you have survived for so long. It is unfortunate that we are on opposite sides. If you had been working for me and not against me there would have been a different outcome.'

'Yeah? You'll have plenty of time to think about that,' Brand said. He gestured with the barrel of his Colt. 'Move.'

Kwo Han hesitated for a fraction of a second. When he did move it was with a terrible speed and a deadly purpose. He took a short step to one side. His right hand slipped inside the open jacket of his suit, and when he withdrew his hand it was grasping the handle of a small hatchet. Kwo Han moved with the agility he had always possessed, and though it had been many years since he had practised the art he found he had lost none of his skills.

Only Brand's acute reflexes warned him of Kwo Han's attack. Even so he was slow in putting up any kind of defense. In the split-second left to him he pulled his body away from the downward slash of the gleaming blade, believing he had avoided it. Dimly he heard Richard Hunt's warning yell. By this time he was bringing up his Colt, lining it up on the angry face before him and jerking back on the trigger. His mind was full of the horror conjured up by the sight of that glinting blade, its keen edge already so close. The reflection of the blade against the bright sun hurt his eyes and he saw images flash into view.

Bare sandy beaches and blue water. Green foliage and the rich red of blood. There was a stunning roar of sound – his Colt going off. Kwo Han's face disintegrating into a bloody mask. And then Brand felt a stunning blow to his skull as the back haft of the hatchet slammed against his skull. Pain exploded inside his head and there was pain so acute it numbed him. He opened his mouth to yell but nothing came out. He knew he was falling. It didn't seem to stop. He sank into a silent, dark void...and after a while he found it wasn't so bad after all...he gave up resisting and let the darkness claim him...he didn't care...it didn't seem important any more...

EPILOGUE

The Confederate gold that had started out from California was never recovered from its resting place on the bed of The Bay of Caves for well over a hundred years. During that time a minor legend grew up around the story of how it found its way to Yucatan, but only a few knew the truth.

Three attempts were made to raise it before the end of the century. They all failed, and those early failures cost four more lives.

The East-West criminal syndicate died along with Kwo Han and the loss of the gold, the impetus draining away. And as Richard Hunt had predicted, Han's organisation also came to an end. Those who evaded arrest soon fell to arguing amongst themselves as to who should take over from the dead Tong Master. They created the seeds of their own destruction.

Major Ruiz rose through the ranks of the *Rurales* and became the youngest ranking officer to command a large district in the Province of Yucatan. His defeat of the bandits who had hired out to Kwo Han had a great influence on the criminal element in and around Agua Verde. The strength of the gangs was considerably weakened and never managed to rise again.

For four days Jason Brand lay unconscious in a small hospital at Agua Verde. Busy as he was with tedious reports he had to compile concerning the Kwo Han affair, and the American and British involvement, Richard Hunt found time to call each day to see how Brand was. So did a young Mexican girl called Angel. On the morning of the fifth day Hunt met the doctor attending Brand outside the American's room.

'I was about to send for you, Captain Hunt.' The doctor was a small, precise Mexican who wore steel-rimmed spectacles and spoke excellent English.

'Has something happened?' Hunt asked.

The doctor nodded. '*Si*. He has recovered consciousness.'

'Can I see him?'

'As long as you do not stay too long. He will need a lot of rest. The blow from that axe is not the only wound I found. *Senor* Brand has been struck a number of times recently. Too many severe blows to the skull can damage the brain. He's lucky to be alive. That final blow he took came near to killing him. If that blade hadn't been deflected slightly and had struck him as intended. He needs plenty of rest to enable him to recover.' The doctor shrugged. 'Well, I do not think I need to explain.'

'Has he said anything yet?'

'No. He was still very tired when he came round. But he has been left alone for a while. Shall we go in?'

Hunt followed the doctor into the small, white-painted room. It was bare save for a single bed and a couple of chairs. An open window looked out onto the neat, quiet garden surrounding the hospital.

Jason Brand lay staring out of the window. His face looked pale and gaunt against the white bandage covering the top of his bead. Dark rings circled his sunken eyes. He looked utterly weary.

'Hello, Jason,' Hunt said. 'How are you feeling?'

Brand turned to look at him, and Hunt was shocked at the empty expression in his eyes.

'*Who're you?*' Brand asked his voice a low monotone.

Hunt glanced at the doctor. 'Doctor?'

The doctor had already moved to Brand's side. '*Senor* Brand, what is wrong?'

'What did you call me? Brand? *Who's Brand?*'

Hunt felt a coldness form in his stomach. He moved to where Brand could see him.

'Jason, don't you know me?'

Brand touched his hand to his head, his face twisting with pain.

'Know you? Hell, why should I know you? I don't even know who I am. Or where I am. So if you know, mister, you'd better tell me.'

Jason Brand will return in
THE KILLING DAYS

A HUNTER BOOKS
Presentation